IT WAITS ON THE TOP FLOOR

BEN FARTHING

BOOKS BY BEN FARTHING

BOOM

THE PIPER'S GRAVEYARD

CROWDED CHASMS

THEY CLING TO THE HULL

1

———

A crooked skyscraper sprung up overnight.

Chris stood in his driveway. November chill seeped through his bathrobe. It was colder than last night, as if the new tower had brought a cold front with it.

Chris loved the simple Richmond skyline, and he knew every angle and window. He'd hoped to design a building for it one day.

This new tower didn't belong. It was off by itself, in Northside somewhere, where it was all neighborhoods. Residential zoning issues weren't quite as eerie as the fact that last night, the building hadn't been there.

Almost as weird: Chris recognized the building. He thought he might have once sketched its twisting tiers, its off-center penthouse.

The tower felt like it belonged to him.

But he'd finished his architecture degrees five years ago, and he'd worked on a grand total of four projects since then. He couldn't place the tugging familiarity of this new building.

"Well?" His wife, Sherri, tapped on the steering wheel in her rumbling Ford. "You chase me out here, beg me to wait, and now what? Your head's right back in the clouds."

Chris looked down at her. He snapped back to his immediate situation. After a night of insomnia, Chris had gone upstairs to find Sherri stuffing clothes into the cherry red Samsonite luggage he'd bought her for Christmas.

It didn't surprise him she was leaving.

But the timing was a kick in the groin—and not just to Chris.

He pulled his bathrobe tight against the cold. He had one chance to sketch out a reason Sherri should stay. Only one angle to take, really. "Did you wake up Eddie to tell him, or am I supposed to break the news?"

Sherri swallowed. She teared up.

Hope flickered inside Chris. Would she change her mind?

"How could you ask me that? This isn't easy for me, either."

"Then don't leave." Chris bit his tongue. He'd let too much exasperation into his voice. Now she'd be mad.

"Tell Eddie I'm sorry. You'll be a good dad. I'm not cut out for this."

Chris resisted the urge to reach for Sherri's hand. The car's heat drifted up to his cheeks. No reason he drew for her would change her mind. He shouldn't have tried at all. Now, he looked like a manipulative loser. He'd never win her back now that she was seeing him like this.

He hated himself for that last thought. "Was your signature on the adoption paperwork even dry before you started the divorce papers?"

Sherri's expression turned sharp. "You should be thanking me. If I'd left when I wanted to, the State wouldn't have finalized the adoption."

Chris leaned back to breathe in the cold, damp air. The new skyscraper grabbed his attention again. It wasn't his design. He was confident in that. But he remembered the scrape of the pencil on drafting paper as he filled in the shadows where the tiers twisted at odd angles. Maybe it'd been an assignment to copy an existing drawing? But even that didn't quite explain why he felt like the tower was his.

"This is why we can't work." Sherri shook her head. "Anything bad happens, you withdraw. What was all that therapy for if you never learned to talk to me?"

Her hypocrisy yanked him back. "Remind me how many times you talked about separation? Help me remember. Was it zero? Zero times?"

"You pushed me into an adoption I wasn't sure about."

"Eddie's been part of our family for three years!"

"On and off. I agreed to be a foster parent, not a permanent mother."

"The paperwork you signed last week says otherwise!"

"You can do this on your own."

"I can't even pay for this house on my own."

"Stop yelling at me."

"Oh, the volume of my voice is the real offense here? Not the fact that now I have to tell Eddie, hey, you know how your bio mom got really into meth after your bio dad died? Well guess what? It's time for another abandonment! So forget the bedroom we painted that garish red color that you love, and the family portrait we took by the river! Forget anything else we did to drill into your little impressionable skull that you're now in a stable home. Because—surprise!—the whole world's shaking again, and the Haberman household is not rated for seismic shocks."

His chest heaved. He watched for Sherri's reaction. He knew later he'd think he'd gone too far, but right now, it was cathartic.

Sherri stared through the windshield. Mascara smudged in the corner of her eyes. "Just mom."

"What?"

"Don't call her Eddie's 'bio mom.' She's just his mom."

A stupid thing to say. Legally, Sherri was now mom. But apparently, she'd never embraced it.

Everything shifted. He'd wanted to woo her back, to persuade her back, to guilt her back. Now, she needed to leave.

Sherri couldn't be here when Eddie woke up. She couldn't have second thoughts and turn around, come back tomorrow and throw Eddie's world back into unstable chaos. She wasn't staying, so she needed to leave forever.

"Get out of my driveway."

He might as well have slapped her. She sobbed and cursed and told him this was his fault.

But she did leave.

His heart pumped like a rattling AC unit. Sweat leaked out of his palms to quickly turn frigid.

His therapist—who Sherri had been paying for, so that was over—suggested he avoid catastrophizing by losing himself in something he loved. Normally, he'd admire the Richmond skyline.

The new building could be his distraction. He should get over there and check it out. Maybe being up close would jog his memory on why he felt possessive of it.

But he was getting ahead of himself.

How the hell had it gone up overnight?

2

EDDIE PEEKED around his bedroom doorframe to watch Sherri leave and Chris follow her outside.

It was his fault, because he hadn't done the right chores.

But maybe there was still time to fix it. Eddie slipped out of his room.

Last night, Eddie pretended to be asleep and then after Chris and Sherri went to bed, he'd snuck out to do some more chores.

He knew perfectly well that adults got angry when you weren't helpful. And you kept them happy by being helpful.

But what adults thought was helpful didn't always make sense. With his old mom, sometimes the best way to be helpful was to sit absolutely still and quiet. But she had problems—that's why he had to leave. And that meant that what she thought was helpful wasn't necessarily what other adults would find helpful.

So Eddie had to guess how Sherri and Chris wanted him to be helpful. At least, if he wanted to stay.

Last night, he'd dusted all the books. Then he heard Chris

coming—sometimes Chris didn't sleep for very long—so Eddie snuck back to bed.

This morning, when he heard them arguing and then Sherri leaving, Eddie knew he'd picked the wrong chore. He hadn't been helpful enough.

Eddie turned in a slow circle, searching the living room for the perfect chore. The books were clean. The fuzzy carpet was vacuumed. The pillows on the couch were stacked just right. The pictures on the walls were crooked.

Eddie started there, and while Chris's shouts drifted in from outside, Eddie decided the walls themselves needed a good scrubbing.

He couldn't reach, and the ladder was in the garage, so he used a rubber band to attach a dishrag to the broom, ran it under the faucet, then got to work.

He started next to the front window.

He heard Chris yelling about money. Sherri had a full-time job, but Chris only worked sometimes. If Sherri left, Eddie didn't know about the rent. His old mom worried about the rent a lot.

Water dripped onto the carpet. Eddie's stomach flipped. His old mom hated it when he spilled.

Outside, the car engine roared. Eddie watched from the window as Sherri backed out of the driveway.

Chris stood watching in his green plaid bathrobe, hands on his hips. He went really still, like his mom's boyfriend did before he started screaming.

Eddie scrubbed the wall harder. "Come on," he said, watching Sherri's car. But no matter how hard he scrubbed, Sherri kept driving. She rounded the corner, disappeared out of sight. Eddie ran to grab another rag to soak up his spills.

But it was too late.

He hadn't been helpful enough.

Sherri was gone.

Eddie squeezed shut his eyes. Some kids his age still cried, but he wanted to act old for his age. That was a big part of being helpful.

Which he'd failed at. Again.

The longer Chris stood still out there, the more Eddie worried. Would he leave, too? Eddie pushed his rag harder into the carpet.

Another car pulled into the driveway. Not Sherri's.

Eddie peeked through the window to see who it was.

3

CHRIS SNAPPED a photo of the building with his phone.

He looked up and down his street to see if any neighbors were out who could confirm what he was seeing.

It had been a total of fourteen hours since Chris had last stood on his porch to repeat his meditative ritual of mentally redesigning the Richmond skyline. He was positive the new building had not been there.

Buildings were not built in fourteen hours.

Steel supports for a building that size took more than a month. He would have been watching it slowly go up.

Actually, he loved Richmond architecture, old and new. Google, in its infinite wisdom, should have suggested news stories about the new building from the day it was proposed.

And he would have felt it going up. It was his, after all.

That didn't make any sense. He must have copied a sketch to a similar building back in school. That was all.

Chris felt himself slipping into this structural mystery. He knew it was an escape just as much as getting drunk would be an escape. There were legitimate problems he needed to deal with.

Rent would be due in three weeks, and that was twelve hundred dollars that he didn't have. Eddie would be awake soon.

Should he send him to school or spend the day together to ease the news? Maybe he should lie to say that Sherri would just be gone for a few weeks, so Eddie could get used to only having Chris around.

No, Eddie was too old for that. Chris would damage the trust between them if he lied.

Okay, so he had to come up with a way to tell Eddie that Sherri was gone without tattooing onto the kid's brain that parents always left.

His hands grew clammy again. His bathrobe practically shuddered from his heartbeat.

He breathed deep and looked at the skyline.

The new building was at least sixty stories, a nose taller than anything else in the Richmond skyline. Its top half was tiered, but unevenly. A narrower fifteen-story section sat atop the bottom twenty stories. Then on top of that, but off-center, another ten stories. At the top, and off-center in the other direction, the final five stories or so.

From this distance, Chris could just barely make out the penthouse on top.

The building itself was glass and steel.

The longer he stared at it, the more he felt like he could figure this all out. He could be a dad. He was already a dad. Legally, he'd been Eddie's permanent dad for just a week, but he'd been his foster dad on and off for three years.

Money was a tougher issue, but he'd come back to that.

Chris stood up. He could research the mystery building later.

Right now, he needed to do everything he could to make their house feel like a permanent home to Eddie.

Thank God at their family photo shoot this week, Sherri had insisted that Eddie take one with just him and Chris.

Oh. That made sense now.

He wished he could tell Sherri to fuck off one more time. What kind of person did that?

No, not right now.

Right now, he was going to get his phone and send the photo of him and Eddie to Walgreens. Once Eddie woke up, they could go pick it up. And then use Sherri's credit card to buy donuts.

He started for the door when a Buick pulled into the driveway.

His first reaction was annoyance that he was still stuck out in the cold in his bathrobe.

Then out stepped the man responsible for Chris's financial problems.

4

CHRIS REALIZED that his anger at Sherri wasn't hate.

This was hate.

Dr. Lance Terry, Chair Professor of Architecture, closed his Buick door and tucked his burgundy leather driving gloves into the pocket of his tweed blazer. The man actually owned driving gloves. Gray, curly hair sat over a pale, intentionally stoic face. He wore thick, saucer-sized glasses that Chris's hipster neighbors were trying to bring back. Dr. Terry never knew they'd left.

He turned a slow circle, taking in the early 1930s squat construction of Chris's rental house. Not a Sears "house-in-a-kit," but the architectural inspiration for them. He raised his eyebrows at Chris, undoubtedly for choosing to live in such an architectural bore. When his slow circle reached the view of Richmond, his shoulders relaxed.

As much as Chris hated Dr. Terry, he understood the love for your own city's skyline.

He noted that Dr. Terry spent only a moment staring at the new lopsided building off in Northside that had shown up overnight. Chris felt a twinge of jealousy. He knew it wasn't his building, but he still didn't want Dr. Terry thinking he could claim it.

Not a useless old fop like him.

Most professors of architecture transitioned to teaching after working in the field. Many had put in time managing actual construction sites. In a hands-on industry, Dr. Terry was one of the few who'd always been an academic. Everything he said sounded like overconfident philosophizing. "From this distance, the city's a mishmash of heartless boxes, but it's *our* mishmash of heartless boxes, is it not?" He finally made eye contact with Chris.

"I've got the same soft spot," Chris said. "But you're right. Not nearly as much personality as, say, Fredericksburg."

Dr. Terry raised his eyebrows. He understood the jab but cared less about the substance and more about the impropriety of it. "Why are you in your bathrobe?"

"I was getting the paper." This was his house. He'd put up with enough shit today. "How do you know where I live?"

"The white pages still exist."

Typical stodgy answer. "Why are you here? Is the college putting tenured professors on fundraising duty now?"

"Hardly. This is outside my scholarly responsibilities."

"A side job?" Chris laughed. It felt good after the morning he'd had. "You think I'd help you with another side job?"

Dr. Terry recoiled. His students didn't laugh at him. His fellow professors treated him with equal respect. He was the preeminent scholar of modern United States architectural history. His recommendation could guarantee a student was accepted to graduate school. His whims could determine whether a visiting professor received tenure or whether a tenured professor received a committee seat. People didn't tell him *no*. They certainly didn't laugh at him.

At seeing Dr. Terry's sagging cheeks tighten in anger, Chris laughed harder, enjoying the moment, pushing out the family disaster lurking in his periphery.

The last time he'd seen Dr. Terry, Chris had been groveling. The culmination of six years of working together, a bachelor's, a master's, and a year of assisting Dr. Terry in designing the twelve-million dollar Fredericksburg courthouse. Chris gathered photographs and sketches of the town's best-known buildings. He personally sketched out ways to bring the town's history of design together into a building that also held a modern sensibility. And to top it off, he outlined ways to make those grandiose designs actually functional. In Dr. Terry's final version, he combined elements of Chris's designs, all polished up with his half-century of experience. It was undeniably Dr. Terry's design, but it also relied on Chris's work.

Chris didn't expect his name to be next to Dr. Lance Terry's in the newspapers, but he at least expected his name to be somewhere down the list on the blueprints.

Instead, Dr. Terry had taken all the credit. When most architectural students were working internships and building their portfolio, Chris was assisting his most respected professor with a job that had nationwide attention. Then he was snubbed, and sent out into the job market with a mild recommendation that said Chris was "particularly astute concerning office tasks."

All because of Chris's unorthodox thesis research. Dr. Terry got embarrassed so he took a wrecking ball to Chris's career.

Chris contained himself.

Dr. Terry smoothed the lapels of his tweed blazer. "This isn't your typical contract work."

The old man honestly thought Chris would work with him. "That's a shame because I've been starving for contract work. In the five years since I graduated, I've had a total of four freelance jobs."

Dr. Terry huffed. "Hardly impressive."

"That's my point. I graduated with no portfolio. I'm broke because you fucked me over."

Dr. Terry let out a mild gasp but then smirked. "Aren't you proud of the four jobs you've completed? That's a portfolio."

"Redesigning stairwells to code? A beach bungalow that the firm charged ten times what they paid me? Not exactly jobs that'll move me up in the world."

"Then you'll want to hear what I have to say."

"I promise you, I don't."

Sure, Chris needed money. But trusting Dr. Terry would leave him with wasted time and an empty wallet.

Dr. Terry cleared his throat. "If you're worried I would somehow cut you out—not that I'm admitting to your version of our last interaction—it may reassure you to hear that your contract would be with my client. Of course, I would hold a managerial role over you, but without the ability to terminate your contract or withhold payment."

That surprised Chris. If the money was guaranteed, could he turn it down? Eddie would wake up any minute. Rent would be due in three weeks. Sherri and her regular paycheck would never be back. Unless Chris wanted to find a cheap apartment and uproot Eddie, he needed money. Hell, he didn't even have the income for a cheap apartment.

Dr. Terry took his hesitation as further resistance. "Perhaps you'd be more eager if I shared with you the job's details?"

Chris tested out cautious optimism. "Couldn't hurt."

Dr. Terry pointed to the Richmond skyline.

No, Chris realized, he was pointing to the right of it, at the new building that had sprung up overnight, a mile north of downtown.

Jealousy returned.

"That's the job," said Dr. Terry. "Our esteemed city's newest addition. I'm sure your fine eye for the obvious made you aware that eyesore wasn't there last night. My client is organizing a team to reverse engineer its construction."

Chris ignored the drab insult. "Reverse engineer?"

Dr. Terry took Chris's surprise for misunderstanding. "You and I are going to figure out how they built it."

5

IT WAS TOO much for one morning. Sherri left. The skyline grew a new building. The man who hijacked Chris's career showed up.

And now that self-serving old fart wanted Chris to "reverse engineer" the impossible tower.

Chris squeezed his jaw to avoid shivering. He needed to get inside. The cold front that arrived with the new tower was too much.

Dr. Terry's forehead wrinkled with impatience. "I thought you'd be more excited. This could be a monumental moment for architecture. Maybe we should step inside?"

"No. I'll warm up in a moment. You can answer my questions out here. Then you can leave."

Dr. Terry tightened his lips. "The contract should answer any questions." Dr. Terry pulled a sheet of crisp, folded paper from his jacket. He handed it to Chris. "I assume compensation is your most pressing question." He gave another judgmental glance at the old rental house.

Chris wanted to laugh. Dr. Terry was judging the rental

house, and with Sherri gone, Chris couldn't even afford that. He'd have to uproot Eddie again.

"Payment is big, yes. Since I can't expect any sort of recommendation from you afterwards."

"Payment is six times the standard for a junior architect with your experience. We expect the job to take three to six hours."

Chris found the dollar figure on the contract. It would cover rent for two months. Even if they still had to move afterwards, it would at least let Eddie stay where he'd been living on-and-off for the past two years. A solid structure until they came to terms with Sherri's abandonment.

Tempting, if Chris could trust the contract. "I take it your client isn't the owner?"

"That's correct."

"Why doesn't your client just ask the owner how they built it?"

"We don't know who it was."

"Pull the permits."

"The only permits on file are for the demolition of the eight houses that used to stand there."

"Ask the demo contractors who paid their invoices."

"My client's legal team is quite capable. The demolition company seems to be on vacation. Bureaucratic avenues are being pursued, have no doubt. But our job is to inspect the new tower with our architectural expertise."

"We're breaking in," Chris realized. A reckless plan. The so-called client was probably just Dr. Terry.

"The paycheck is worth the risk of a minor misdemeanor."

"That's a good news story, huh? 'Architecture professor

breaks into mysterious building.' Everyone in the industry will know your name."

"They already do."

Chris ground his teeth. He should share a tiny portion of Dr. Terry's reputation. But right now, he could really use six times the normal rate. He swallowed his pride. It went down like a lump of cement.

Chris realized his hesitation wasn't just about pride. He still didn't trust the offer. "Who's your client?"

"They prefer to remain anonymous until you sign the contract."

It was definitely Dr. Terry. Chris was out. There was no actual opportunity for a paycheck here.

But money wasn't the only thing on Chris's mind. "What do you know about the building already? Did it really go up overnight?"

"We can't yet find any security cameras trained on it. But we're quite positive that it was not there last night, and it was there this morning."

Chris could confirm that. He'd stood on the porch last night and hadn't seen it. "What's the government think?"

"If they've noticed, they're slow to act."

"And the news?"

"Nothing on the morning news shows. But once they realize what's happened, I imagine they'll act quickly. So we need to move faster. We'll meet my client in half an hour at the Steelside Cafe."

Chris nodded. He desperately wanted to know how the building went up so fast. This was a breakthrough in construction like jumping from mud huts to steel framing. But Dr. Terry didn't have any answers for him. All that was left was to torment his old adversary a bit. "And what's your plan to reverse engineer it?"

Dr. Terry was an ivory tower academic. He knew the history of architecture, and he could design buildings that mimicked any historical style. But he wasn't a construction manager. Chris would be surprised if Dr. Terry could even walk someone through the process of constructing a skyscraper, let alone reverse engineer irregular construction.

"That's part of why I've come to you. For my own part, I rub shoulders with our generation's leading architects. I know their work intimately. Our primary approach will be to review the design both inside and out. That should give me enough information to determine who has designed this building. Once I have that information, our client can go to that architect to inquire as to the construction methods."

It was so stupid it made Chris happy. "It's an office building, not an *avant-garde* single-family home. No way the design is distinct enough."

Dr. Terry tugged at his jacket. "I'm quite confident in my abilities."

"That's the truth."

Chris looked past the skyline. The new tower seemed to shrug with each tier. It was glass from corner to corner. "Any freshman student could have designed that thing." Maybe that's what it was. Had one of his classmates designed it, and Chris recognized their work?

No, because Dr. Terry would have noticed, and he'd be bothering someone else this morning.

But examining the design was the only approach Dr. Terry had. The old man knew nothing about actual construction. Chris didn't know a lot, but he had spent summers during undergrad doing the grunt labor for the Bank of America building downtown. And he kept in touch with a lot of friends who'd gone on to various engineering and construction management positions.

"Perhaps you have some suggestions on other approaches we could take in finding out who built this and how."

"Sure." Now Chris was just dragging along Dr. Terry in order to avoid going inside. "If we just find the-"

He stopped. He'd thought of a solid way to get answers about the construction. Better than staring at the building and then guessing the architect. But he wasn't about to make Dr. Terry's job any easier.

"What is it?" Dr. Terry leaned closer. "You've thought of something."

"Wouldn't you know, it just slipped my mind. I should really get back to my *office tasks*."

"Don't be daft. I'm offering you a handsome paycheck."

"Ha! *You're* offering me. There's no client."

"What?" Dr. Terry sputtered. "Of course there is. You think I'd choose to work with you again after the embarrassment you brought to your alma mater?"

"Oh fuck off. I was a nineteen-year-old kid caught up in an exciting story. You demoed my career because deep down, you know you're a mediocre architect propping up his career with articles nobody reads."

"And you'd have done better without my tutelage?"

"Without your assholery, yes!"

Dr. Terry's cheeks went red before an idea sparked in his eyes. "I see what's going on. You want to do it without me. You've somehow heard about the open contract. Who told you? One of your college chums who gave up on designing?"

Chris had no idea what he was talking about but sensed another opportunity to jab at the old man. "Why would I admit to that?"

"No one will be collecting the open contract because the private team will get the answer first. I should know, since I'm leading the private team!"

Chris took a moment to digest Dr. Terry's blubbering. Maybe there really was a client. And while they'd hired Dr. Terry to reverse engineer the new building, they'd also posted an open reward.

"The client must not have much faith in you."

Dr. Terry breathed deep. He sucked in mustache hairs. "I'm offering you guaranteed payment. If you go after the open contract, you'll get nothing."

"Sorry," said Chris, gleeful at how easy it was to manipulate Dr. Terry's emotions. "I'm at the point in my career where I need to take risks. And if that screws you out of this cash and prestige that you're looking for, well, I'm sure you can fall back on other accolades. Office tasks, maybe."

"You can't-"

"Of course, I'll need to verify that this open contract exists." He checked the time on his phone. "You said your client will be at the Steelside at nine-thirty, right?"

"That's a private meeting-"

"I'll only interrupt for a second. I'll see you there. Now get out of my driveway."

Dr. Terry huffed back into his Buick and left.

His fun over, the weight of the day fell back onto Chris's shoulders.

He had no intention of chasing after any contracts.

If it had been anybody but Dr. Terry, then Chris could

have trusted the contract and set out on a breaking-and-entering adventure. But it was Dr. Terry, and whether he was the client or the manager, he'd find a way to screw Chris out of payment.

Of course, he wanted to know more about the tower. Everything there was to know. It was *his*, somehow.

But so was Eddie. And Eddie was far more important than professional curiosity. Today would be about lessening the blow of another parent abandoning him.

Chris turned his back on the skyline, pulled his bathrobe tight around him, and walked inside to break the news to his son.

6

Eddie watched and listened through a cracked window.

Eddie cracked the window to hear.

Chilled air seeped inside. Soapy water had dripped onto his hands which now felt icy cold.

Outside, Chris argued with an old man. The old man dressed like someone on the British mystery shows on PBS.

Except Chris liked watching those. Eddie had never seen Chris so angry as he was at this old man.

Eddie went back to scrubbing the walls. He'd already messed up and made Sherri leave. He'd make sure he was helpful enough so Chris wouldn't leave, too.

Still, he listened.

There was a new building, and the old man wanted Chris to find something inside. It sounded like it was worth a lot of money.

That was good news. Maybe Chris wouldn't have to worry about rent money.

Chris yelled even louder, and then the old man slammed his car door and drove away.

Chris headed inside.

Eddie slid the window shut as quietly as he could.

The front door opened. Chris came through, hugging his bathrobe to his chest. He was skinnier than when Eddie had first met him, three years ago during first grade. But this morning, his eyes weren't wide and worried like they usually were. There was still some anger in the way Chris's teeth pushed against each other. But Eddie knew it wasn't for him.

Chris looked at the broom with the wet rag lashed on with a rubber band. "What's all this?"

"Cleaning the walls," Eddie said. "Is that man giving you a job?"

"No." Chris exhaled. "Let me get dressed, and then let's make breakfast and have a conversation."

"About Sherri leaving?"

"You saw? Yeah, about Sherri leaving."

Eddie understood *leaving*. But he didn't understand this job Chris had turned down. "It sounded like he was giving you a job. Wouldn't a job be helpful?"

"Sure, if it's legit."

"Looking around in a new building isn't legit?"

"Dr. Terry isn't legit." Chris sat on the couch to get to eye level with Eddie. "Why are you so concerned about this job?"

"It'd be helpful," Eddie repeated. Sometimes adults didn't realize the connection between helpfulness and how nice they were. "Plus you're always looking for more jobs."

"Not like this one. The old guy out there, he wanted me to search all over a new building, and if I found what I was looking for, he wasn't planning on sharing."

"Like a treasure hunt?"

Chris smiled. "Exactly. Never go treasure hunting with a greedy partner."

"Like in our game." Eddie pointed to the TV. They played Treasure Hunter X together, and even though it was older than the games his friends at school played, he still liked it.

"Yeah, I guess it is like Treasure Hunter X." Chris blinked slowly. He was thinking about Sherri, Eddie could tell. "Sure would be helpful to have some of that treasure, huh?"

Eddie nodded. *Helpful.*

"Listen, let's both get dressed, and then we'll make pancakes. I need to tell you a few things about Sherri." He gave him a quick hug, then went to his bedroom. Rock music drifted through the closed door.

Eddie hurried to put on his shoes and find his warmest coat.

He had a chance to be more helpful than ever.

There was treasure in the new building. Chris said it'd be helpful to have it.

If Eddie could get it for him, Chris would never leave.

While Chris got dressed to angry rock songs, Eddie left a quick note on the kitchen table, then snuck outside.

He'd find the treasure. The new building was waiting.

7

CHRIS LAY FULLY DRESSED on his unmade bed.

Sherri's stereo systems pumped out *The 1975*. He didn't care for their jangly melodies, but it was the last thing Sherri had playing from the iPad.

He had to get up.

Eddie needed him.

But now, he and Eddie lived in an empty house.

He didn't want to open the door and confront it.

All his determination to help Eddie feel at home was just so overwhelming. He couldn't do it alone. Not that he'd have to do it if he weren't alone.

Seven years with Sherri down the drain.

Sherri hadn't taken much with her. Last year, she'd hauled away all her belongings that didn't "spark joy" to try out a minimalist lifestyle. Chris only joined in the minimalism inasmuch as he felt awkward spending Sherri's paycheck on personal stuff. And on the few times he earned his own paycheck, he was most excited to pay rent for a month.

Their bedroom was simple but quality Hayne's furniture. Out in the front room, the dining table had been a Facebook Marketplace find. The chapter books on the shelf had been accumulated over the past three years since Eddie had become part of their lives. He picked them up one at a time, for fifty cents each at the Church Hill Library book sales. Now that he thought about it, Sherri had never bought a single one.

Chris expected to feel distraught. The emptiness that came instead hit like a sucker punch.

Tears would come. Ugly, snotty tears.

But this emptiness threatened to swallow everything.

It had the same flavor as four years of career failure.

Last summer, after he'd completed the beach cottage design, his therapist subtly dropped the word "situational" from Chris's "situational depression." He felt empty and numb and Sherri leaving was just more numbness.

And now he was in an empty house full of Sherri's things.

The couch where he laid his head on Sherri's lap while they watched *The Great British Baking Show*. The counter where Sherri cooked a hazelnut and chocolate licqueur birthday cake and sang to Chris by herself. The table where Chris set Sherri's sunny-side-up egg on wheat toast each morning, before she went off to calculate risk for State Farm drivers.

But those memories were numb. He thought that in this moment, he should be desperately pining to fry an egg and season it with his tears while he wished he could serve it to Sherri one last time. Or watch British people make "biscuits" so he could hear Sherri cooing over the playful piping.

But he didn't. Her leaving stabbed him in a place that was already empty.

Chris rolled over.

He'd run a couple half-marathons as a teenager. The effort it took to push hard that last few miles was nothing compared to the effort it took to get up off that bed.

But he did it.

And with that momentum, he left the bedroom.

"Eddie? Do you want chocolate chips in your pancakes?" It'd be one more task to add those, but he could commit now and then force himself to do it afterwards.

Chris pushed aside thoughts of Sherri to pull the skillet from the cabinet and set it on the stove. "Eddie?"

The house was too quiet. Chris walked back down the hallway. Eddie's bedroom door was open. Nobody inside.

He went back to the front room. Eddie's shoes weren't by the door. His coat wasn't on the rack.

Chris stuck his head out the front door. A neighbor a few doors down was pulling out of their driveway. But Eddie wasn't out there.

Chris stood in the living room. He breathed deep. There was no need to panic. He looked around the room.

Three years ago, he'd sat on this couch with a nervous lump in his gut the day CPS had brought Eddie over for the first time. He'd crouched down to embrace the underweight six-year-old. Eddie glared like Chris was the one who'd uprooted him, but he relaxed a little when he saw his race-car bed, freshly painted with Dale Earnhardt Jr.'s number.

There at the kitchen table, Chris had cried tears of confusion when CPS said Eddie could go home to his birth mother *again*.

There was the low spot in the carpet from Chris pacing for three months, worrying about Eddie, already knowing that the state's attempt to send him back home would never work out.

There was the brown stain on the carpet by the TV from when they'd ordered Vocelli's with extra cheese because Eddie was back again, but in the three months he'd been gone, he'd lost twelve pounds.

There was the shelf full of chapter books that Chris read out loud at night. At first, Eddie complained he could read himself and that Chris's voices would only be funny to a five-year-old. Now he giggled when Chris attempted a French accent while reading *Harry Potter and the Goblet of Fire*.

There was the old 32-bit console under the TV that Chris had found at a yard sale, on which he and Eddie had spent countless Friday evenings.

Where was Sherri in any of those memories? Nearby, surely. But not involving herself enough to be cemented in his memory.

Thinking of Eddie gave substance to the empty space that swallowed Sherri's dagger. Not properly, not completely, but it centered him.

A small corner of his mind recognized he wasn't being fair to Sherri. He walled it off. He needed the anger to avoid collapsing into a pile of defeat.

Chris breathed deeply again.

Eddie was probably just in the bathroom.

Chris went to knock, but on the way he found a note on the kitchen table. It was scrawled in a fourth-grader's crooked, looping lettering.

I'll find the treasure.

No. Chris felt panic blossoming in his chest. He tried to reassuring himself.

It was just breaking-and-entering. It would probably be a slap on the wrist for a 9-year-old. More likely Chris would face greater legal jeopardy for letting him out of his sight.

So why did Chris feel like Eddie had jumped headfirst into a snakepit?

That was stupid. He didn't know how it went up overnight, but it was just a building. No need to panic.

He'd just catch up to Eddie and bring him home.

Chris jogged back outside. With his coat, this time.

He ran to the corner but didn't see Eddie. How far could the kid have got in ten minutes?

If Chris hadn't spent so long lying on his bed, this wouldn't have happened.

He needed to bring him home.

Chris suddenly remembered dropping Eddie back off with the social worker. He'd been afraid of what his bio mom —or her boyfriend—might do this time. So he downloaded a ride-sharing app to Eddie's phone and added his credit card.

Chris pulled up his credit card app, and sure enough, there was the pending charge.

Eddie was taking an Uber to the impossible skyscraper.

Chris grabbed his keys to go after his son.

8

EDDIE HOPPED out of the Uber. He left a big tip with Chris's credit card. He had to promise that for the driver to pick him up since he was just a kid.

It was normal houses around him. They were old like his old mom's house but clean and bright like Chris's house.

He craned his neck to look up at the office building in front of him. It was clean, too, but not bright. It felt cold, like the chilly November morning was only chilly because the building was like an inside-out refrigerator.

To Eddie, this new building was creepier than the rest of the city.

He had the strange thought that this building wasn't *for* him. But buildings were just places. They were *for* whoever worked in them.

The angles and corners were all "janky" like Mom would say. It looked like someone had a done a bad job stacking up the toy blocks that Chris bought him the first time Eddie stayed over. Even though they were little kid toys, Eddie liked getting the present.

The whole side of the building was glass windows. Mirrors that showed the cloudy sky.

He never knew they could build a skyscraper like this so fast.

His phone buzzed. Probably Chris texting again. Eddie ignored it. As long as he didn't look at the texts, he wouldn't see Chris telling him to stop and come home.

But he looked enough to check that they were from Chris.

Chris had changed the contact name to "Dad."

Eddie liked calling him "Dad," when he remembered to.

That's why he was here, after all.

Sherri left because Eddie's chore this morning wasn't good enough.

The man that Chris—Dad—was talking to afterwards said that Dad had to find the money inside the new building, or Dad couldn't keep the house.

Eddie had already messed up today. Made it all a "cluster" like Mom used to say, except she'd also say that other word Eddie wasn't allowed to say.

He made the house a cluster, and so Sherri couldn't see that he was helpful. That's why she left.

And now Dad needed the treasure that the old man said was inside this new building. But Dad didn't want to get it.

So Eddie would get it for him. It was the best chore he'd ever thought of. He'd be so helpful that Chris would want to be his dad forever.

He knew it wasn't really money inside, like a suitcase full of dollar bills. It'd be something that cost a lot of money. Treasure. A whole box full of Nintendo Switches, or maybe jewelry like in the glass counter at the pawn shop that had $1 DVDs.

Now that he wouldn't see his old mom anymore, he wondered if Chris would still take him to the pawn shop.

He leaned his neck way back to look up at the tippy top of the building.

It was farther up than he could see.

Eddie got a butterfly in his belly. Not a happy one, like before the pizza guy knocked on the door. But a yucky one, like the time Mom found his rock collection in the closet.

This building was huge.

Maybe he should just go home. If he did a bunch of small chores, Dad would still see how useful he was.

But then he'd have to explain why he used the Uber account that was only for emergencies.

As long as it took, Eddie had started this big chore. He'd have to find the treasure.

It wouldn't be so hard. It was just like the third stage of Treasure Hunter X for Dad's Playstation. Sneak in and grab the treasure.

He just had to find a way in the first floor. Then check all the hiding spots. The treasure moved each time you played, but Eddie knew all the spots it could be.

He hoped the front door was unlocked.

He looked across the street at the bottom floor. A teenage girl was peeking in through the glass door.

Eddie felt some relief. He didn't want to explore this building by himself.

"Hey," he yelled, hurrying over, "I can help you."

The girl jumped. She spun around, then laughed when she saw Eddie.

He stopped. Did he look funny?

She had a wheezy laugh. Her braided hair click-clacked.

"Ooh boy, you scared the shit out of me. You move real quiet, you know that?"

"Yeah." Eddie was the best at sneaking. "Do you want to look for the treasure together? I have to find it for my Dad."

She raised an eyebrow. "How'd you get here? The only white families for six blocks don't have any kids your age. You just move in?"

"No."

"Your parents let you play with friends in Barton Heights?"

"What's that?"

"The neighborhood you're standing in. The proudest neighborhood in Richmond. Lowest crime rate in Northside. Highest property values. The one black neighborhood they couldn't destroy."

Eddie knew she meant that black people lived here, but the houses were so colorful, it was weird to call it black.

"What's the matter? Forget how to speak?"

"No, I remember. At my old house when I lived with Mom my friend Tommy was black."

"You're what? Eight years old, already talking about 'My best friend is black.'" She raised her eyebrow and laughed again.

"I'm nine."

"What's your name?"

"Eddie. What's yours?"

"Cam. You don't live with your mom no more, Eddie?"

He shook his head. "I live with Chris now. Sherri left today since I wasn't helpful enough, and I think Chris can't pay rent unless he finds the treasure the man in the driveway told him about..."

He noticed that Cam was smiling with her mouth open now.

"One thing at a time. First, why are you talking to me?"

"I can help you. Are you looking for the treasure, too?"

"We'll come back to that. Who's Chris? Do you like him? Is he nice?"

Those were the sort of questions that Mrs. Vicky at school asked him when he first stayed with Chris. "He said I can call him Dad."

"Yeah, they tell you that. I hope you got a good one. When I was your age, my Mom got a shitty boyfriend, so I got sent to foster homes for a year. Then she kicked him out and I went back home." Cam breathed in quickly. "But that doesn't always happen. Don't get your hopes up, I mean."

"They said Chris is my dad now. I used to see my old mom sometimes, but I won't anymore."

"At least he's nice." Cam looked back through the glass doors. "Your new dad, he knows about this building?"

"He designs buildings. But I don't think this one. The man in the driveway just said he has to find the treasure inside."

"You know this wasn't here last night."

"Yeah." Eddie pressed his face against the glass next to Cam. Inside was a dark room with a bunch of doors. Little windows in each door were lit up. The real inside must be on the other side.

"What do you mean by 'treasure'?" Cam asked.

"I don't know. Maybe gold coins. Or like a dead pirate's sword with diamonds on the handle."

"How do you know there's treasure inside?"

"The man in the driveway said it'd pay for Dad's house."

Cam nodded. "It's a big building. Do you know where this treasure is supposed to be?"

Eddie had memorized every hiding spot in Treasure Hunter X. This would be the same. "I know all the hiding places it might be."

"Because the man in the driveway told you?"

"He didn't tell me anything," Eddie said. "I was being sneaky and listening. He was talking to my dad."

"That's what's up. You sneaky as hell."

Eddie felt proud. "I'm helpful, too."

Cam crouched down. "I'm not a specialist or anything, but you talk a lot about being helpful. Your mom did a number on you, huh?"

He looked at his shoes. He shook his head. "I like being helpful."

"You'll learn when you're older that you don't have to go crazy for other people. You can be the shit all on your own. Hell, look at me."

Eddie looked up. "Is shit good?" He felt a little thrill at saying a bad word.

Cam threw her head back and laughed. "*The* shit. Like, 'you the man.'"

Eddie nodded. He understood what she meant, but she was wrong. Even though she was older than him, she wasn't an adult. Adults wanted you to be helpful.

He changed the subject. "Are you looking for the treasure, too? We can split it. We save my dad's house, and you can have the rest."

"I gotta look for my own treasure first. This was an empty lot yesterday. My mom's got another new boyfriend and he's always stealing from my purse. So I got a hundred-eighty dollars buried next to a rock somewhere in there. That's halfway to affording this real estate class, so I can have a real job as soon as I'm eighteen."

"I can help you find it." Eddie searched the grass between the building and the road. He didn't see any rocks.

"No, it was in the middle of the lot. Then this skyscraper appeared last night. So my money's gotta be in the basement or somewhere. At least, I hope. You tag along, and then after we find my real estate money, you can show me where this treasure is."

Eddie felt a big smile coming on. Cam saw how helpful he was. Now he didn't have to go treasure hunting by himself. This building was creepier than the one in Treasure Hunter X.

Because it wasn't *for* him.

That was a weird thing to think.

Eddie pushed the thought from his mind.

"Is it unlocked?" he asked. He pulled on the handle. It didn't budge. "Nope."

Cam tried it, and the door swung open. Comfortable heat drifted out into the chill September day. "Let's go find our treasure."

"Wait," Eddie pulled out his phone. He opened his text messages. He still avoided reading Dad's messages, but he typed and sent: *I'm going inside to get the treasure. I'll text you after.* He tucked his phone back into his pocket.

"Okay, I'm ready."

Cam patted Eddie's shoulder and led the way inside.

9

———

CHRIS'S rusty Chevy rattled up the interstate.

He ignored speed limits, but it was rush hour, so he could only go so fast. He wished he knew how far ahead Eddie was. That depended on how long Chris had been lying on the bed, which he wasn't sure of.

I-95 swung him around downtown, and the new skyscraper came into view ahead.

It was blocky, like Brutalist era design. But predominantly glass, like the International Style which was on its way out due to terrible cooling efficiency. Its tiers rejected any regular progression in their sizes, which fit with postmodern designs.

Chris was grasping at straws.

It was a hodgepodge of architectural eras. Dr. Terry's plan to figure out the architect was nonsense. Today's leading architects were all about going green. That, and architectural psychology. Design the outside for energy efficiency. Design the inside to motivate, calm, excite, or whatever the purpose of the building was.

Nothing like this impossible tower.

Chris's phone buzzed.

Finally, a text from Eddie. But Chris's relief was short-lived.

I'm going inside to get the treasure. I'll call you after.

Frantic again, Chris texted back, one eye on the road. *There's no treasure!*

He waited for the his text to be marked "delivered." It didn't happen.

He was too late. Eddie had gone inside, and the new building was blocking cell service.

Chris stomped the accelerator to pass a slow truck, then had to swerve back over to make his exit.

He didn't have an address for the tower, but he could see it.

He was in Northside somewhere. An old black neighborhood they'd chopped in half with the interstate.

Normally, he'd be inching along, admiring the architecture. Today, he didn't notice it.

A couple wrong turns and circling back around blocks, and he found the new building.

It took up most of a block. Chris didn't take time to admire it. He parked on the street and hopped out.

That jealous feeling of ownership flooded back through him. From this low angle, the building filled the sky. Glass sides reflected the gray sky.

Chris ran to the doors. Locked. He shook the handles.

It couldn't be locked. Eddie had got inside.

He wouldn't have locked the door behind him, would he?

Chris jogged around to the next side of the building. No doors here, so he ran on to the opposite side. His lungs burned with the cold air.

He wanted to step back and inspect every detail of this impossible skyscraper, but first he had to stop Eddie.

He found an identical bank of doors, also locked.

He pounded his fist against the glass and shouted Eddie's name.

He cupped his hands on the door to look through. He could see another bank of doors. It was a vestibule to keep the inner doors from opening directly to the outside, two layers of doors meant to isolate the inside temperature from the outside. Now it was isolating Chris from his son.

He stepped back and looked for something to break the glass.

Nothing but the cement walkway and landscaping beds waiting for mulch.

He walked back to the street. There had to be something. The old Victorian revival homes were well kept and painted in bright colors. But their landscaping was grass—no stone planters that could smash a glass door.

Chris took a breath.

This wasn't the smartest choice.

He should talk to Dr. Terry. Maybe the old professor could get Chris inside.

No wait, Dr. Terry didn't have another way in. He'd said he planned on breaking in, too.

Breaking in was the best option, then.

Chris peered around the neighborhood but didn't see anyone outside. He could ask if anyone saw Eddie, but he didn't need confirmation to know that Eddie did what Eddie intended.

The boy worried too much about keeping the house

clean, but when he decided to get something done, he couldn't be diverted.

Eddie was in that building.

Chris needed to get him out.

And not just to avoid the breaking-and-entering charge, but because the building was *impossible.*

It couldn't have gone up overnight, and yet it did. Something inside had broke every rule of construction, and Chris didn't know if it was structurally sound, or otherwise dangerous.

It did feel dangerous. The possessive urge remained, but now that the building loomed over him, it gave off an unnatural aura. If it was his, he didn't want it, and he damn well didn't want his son inside.

He walked back around the building. He couldn't find one single goddamn loose brick. Not even a heavy branch.

That wasn't the best way to break in, anyways. He'd probably cut his hand open and then be stuck getting stitched while Eddie wandered a dangerous skyscraper.

There was a Home Depot not far from here. He could get a crowbar, come back, and force a door open.

He looked once more for something that could break a window. Nothing.

Chris jumped in his car and raced away.

10

————

CHRIS WAS in and out in five minutes. Since he still had Sherri's credit card, he didn't limit himself to the crowbar. He didn't know where in that unnatural building Eddie had got to. He grabbed everything he imagined might be useful for forcing his way through an office building. Then he charged them all to Sherri's Visa and jumped back into the car.

He pulled up his phone's GPS to make sure he had the fastest way back.

The Steelside Cafe was on the way.

That's where Dr. Terry originally said to meet him.

It was a big building. It wouldn't hurt to ask Dr. Terry's crew to keep an eye out for Eddie.

And Chris could see if Dr. Terry actually had a client, or was on his own mission.

Chris could be in and out in two minutes.

With that decided, he drove to the Steelside Cafe and parked between a Tesla Model S and a Land Rover.

So, this was an upper-crust sort of sandwich shop.

Sherri would chide him for criticizing wealth. Some

people worked hard. Others were lucky. We don't need to hate them for it.

Sure, but that didn't mean he had to feel comfortable around them.

He got out of the car.

He'd actually heard of The Steelside Cafe since it had a raving review on *Good Eats*. It was a two-story colonial house converted into a restaurant after the busy Hermitage Road was rezoned commercial. It was the hottest new joint in Lakeside, one neighborhood over from the impossible tower.

Chris watched a bearded man in a leather jacket walking his labradoodle spot the building, hesitate, snap a photo with his phone, then keep walking.

A sixty-story skyscraper had shown up in a mostly residential area of town, but dogs still had to shit. Folks had to go to work. And eat.

Chris walked inside the cafe. A bell jangled. He breathed in the smell of fresh bread.

A short line of people waited at the counter for coffee and croissants. A dozen tables took up the seating area, half occupied. The restaurant was small enough that even a little conversation created a cramped din.

Chris scanned the room for Dr. Terry. Chris had somehow beat him here. Or Dr. Terry had lied about the meeting place or moved it out of fear that Chris would crash it.

He felt a surge of panic. If Dr. Terry lied about this, what else did he lie about? How dangerous was the new building? And now he'd wasted time by stopping here.

Then Chris saw a familiar face. Dr. Terry wasn't lying about having a wealthy client.

He'd seen her on TV and in dozens of news articles. It had to be her.

Micah Rayner.

She was tall and slender. Shoulder-length hair that had been fiery red was now fading to white. She ate an English muffin sandwich with a fork and knife.

She sat at the table in the window with two men, who Chris didn't care about yet. Micah Rayner was a goddamn celebrity. Chris had applied for an internship at one of her firms but hadn't even been invited to the first round of interviews. She was doing for construction what Henry Ford had done for automation or what John Browning had done for the rifle.

Chris thought of a million questions to ask her. *Was Elon Musk angry when your solar panel roof doubled his power output? Do you expect your fire control system to be adopted for residential use? What was your secret construction project at the White House?*

Any other time, Chris would geek out at meeting this tech and construction billionaire. But today, he needed a simple favor.

He walked up, thrust out his hand. "Hi Micah, I'm-"

One of the men he'd ignored grabbed Chris's wrist and slammed it against the table, which scraped and screeched against the floor. Orange juice and coffee splashed onto the tabletop.

The man's grip was like a vice squeezing Chris's bones together.

Chris twisted his neck to get a look at him.

He was a skyscraper himself. Only fawning over celebrity had caused Chris to miss him. Sitting down, he could look

Chris level in the eyes. Beard stubble did a poor job of covering scars under his eye and below his lip. Cauliflower ear suggested that when he wasn't protecting Micah from handshakes, he was fighting people for fun, maybe in a boxing ring, probably in a back alley.

"Who are you?" he growled.

Micah answered for him. "This must be Chris Haberman. Dr. Terry went to fetch him. Where is Dr. Terry?" She spoke softly but firmly. "Let go of his wrist, Roberts."

Roberts released Chris. He drank deeply from his steaming coffee cup. Chris rubbed his sore wrist and made a mental note to avoid sudden movements.

"Have a seat," Micah gestured to an open seat between Roberts and the other man Chris hadn't paid attention to yet. "This is Leon."

This last man was closer to Chris's size. He sported buzzed hair and a blond beard down to his chest. His camou-flage coat looked odd next to Roberts' wool sailor's peacoat, and Micah's leather jacket. Leon chewed a donut with his mouth open. He winked at Chris when he caught him star-ing. Chris nodded a hello.

Chris looked back to Micah. "I've turned down Dr. Terry's offer, but I need to ask a favor." As the words came out of his mouth, he felt like an idiot. Turn down a job with Micah Rayner?

"It wasn't your old mentor's offer." Micah patted her mouth with a handkerchief. "It was mine."

"I guess I should reconsider, but honestly, I'm looking at bigger things right now."

She held up her hand. "You'd prefer the open contract. Dr. Terry mentioned that."

Oh yeah. He'd said that to the old man to piss him off.

Roberts huffed like a rhinoceros and eyed Chris like he were a rodent about to be stomped. "Selfish and stupid."

"Enterprising," offered Leon. He wiped coffee from his mouth with a camouflage sleeve.

"No, I-"

Micah cut him off again. "Your decision surprised me, based on Dr. Terry's description of you. I imagined that a failed architect with raw talent and unorthodox interests would be a model employee, but here you are beaming with entrepreneurial spirit. Why aren't you a broken man, Mr. Haberman?"

If she was interviewing him for a job, it was the oddest question he'd ever heard. "Well first off, fuck Dr. Terry. He sabotaged my portfolio out of grad school. Blows my mind why he'd recommend me to you now. Either way, a slow start to my career isn't enough to *break* me."

"I see that. The question is why?"

"I've got responsibilities." Eddie needed stability. And to get the hell out of that building.

"Many broken men put food on their tables. I'd still expect you to be more resigned to failure."

"I've got bigger problems than money right now. I came to ask-"

"Still dancing around my question."

This cutting him off was getting annoying. "What is this crazy shit? I don't want your job. If Dr. Terry's involved, he'll find a way to fuck me over."

Micah's gaze went sharp, and Chris remembered that she commanded multi-billion dollar organizations.

"Watch your tone," growled Roberts.

Leon swatted Roberts' arm. "Easy there, big guy. Let them haggle out their agreement."

Chris took a breath. "I'm sorry. I only stopped by because I know you're going in that building, and my son heard me turn down Dr. Terry's offer, so now he's run off to break in himself. He thinks there's a treasure inside."

Leon clapped once. "I like this kid. He sees what he wants and—bam!—goes after it."

"You don't know the half of it," Chris said. "So the only reason I'm here is to ask you to keep an eye out for him while you're in there."

Micah ran her finger along the lip of her cup. "Why does your son think there's treasure in the building?"

"He misunderstood Dr. Terry's offer. Instead of searching the building to reverse engineer it and then get paid, he thought I'd be searching for something valuable."

"You would be," said Micah. "In a sense."

"You know what I mean."

"If I'm understanding you correctly," Micah said, "you received a job offer paying six times the going rate, and instead turned it down to pursue the related open contract. But you've since changed your mind and are now only here to ask that we search for your truant son?"

"More or less, yeah."

"You've struggled to launch your career, correct? And you do know who I am? Why aren't you leaping at this opportunity?"

She was right. Or she would be if Eddie hadn't run off. "It's just been a hell of a morning."

Leon exaggerated a scoff. "I bet mine was worse. Two flat tires!"

"My wife left me," Chris said, "one week after we finalized the adoption of our son."

Leon hissed. "Ouch."

A weight collapsed on Chris's shoulders. It was Roberts patting his back. The giant gave a supportive, painful squeeze and then went back to his coffee. "I don't wish that grief on anybody. It's good you're staying focused on your boy."

Micah's bodyguard was an emotional cheerleader. Not what Chris expected.

"Perhaps you'd like another opportunity to accept my offer," Micah said. "If even your son has noticed your financial stress, then you must be desperate for money."

Chris ground his molars, trying to think. Every second he waited here, Eddie got deeper into the building. "I still don't trust Dr. Terry."

"Your contract would be with me."

"If I'm working with him, he'll find a way to screw me over."

Roberts said to Micah, "Let him pursue the open contract. He's too distracted to be an effective member of our team."

Micah rubbed her chin. "I'd prefer he be nearby."

"Why?" Chris asked. "Why me?"

"I was impressed with Dr. Terry's description of you."

That was hard to believe, but Chris didn't see why Micah would lie about it. The more he thought about her offer, the more it made sense. He was heading inside anyways to get Eddie. "I'll go after the open contract."

Now Micah asked, "Why?"

"For the money."

"There's something else."

"What do you care?"

"Tell me why you want the job."

Chris took a breath. She'd pried open the floodgates, so he'd give her what she wanted. "I need to pay rent. Eddie— my boy—got passed around from his bio mom to aunts and uncles to grandparents, even before he entered the foster care system. Then two years of adding my wife and me into the carousel of instability, and right when the judge finally says, 'slow down, let's keep the ground steady under the kid's feet,' his new adoptive mom takes off. And she takes her regular paycheck with her. I need rent money, because Eddie needs a permanent home." Chris jammed his tongue between his teeth to keep from grinding them. He didn't even like being that open with Sherri, let alone a table of strangers. But Micah had forced it out of him.

Micah shook her head. "That's why you need money. Why do you want to enter this building?"

Because it's mine, Chris thought. But he said, "To get my son out before he gets arrested. And the money for a stable home."

Micah locked eyes with him. Somehow, she knew he was lying.

She looked at Roberts. "What do you think?"

Chris reevaluated Roberts' position. Bodyguard, emotional cheerleader, and consultant?

"He's dealing with anxiety, grief, and years of doubting himself. I think he needs this tower job."

Something about the way Roberts phrased that caught Chris's attention. Chris needed any job. What did this specific job have to do with Chris's situation?

Micah pinched her brow. She wasn't satisfied with

Roberts' answer, either. She seemed to be hunting for something inside Chris. He didn't like it.

"You can pursue the contract," Micah said.

Roberts pulled a briefcase out from under the table, opened it, and handed Chris the top sheet of a stack of identical forms. There at the top: $200,000.

That would keep Eddie safe and steady. How had he stumbled into such luck?

It wasn't luck. Dr. Terry had recommended him.

But it'd still be up to Chris to actually get it done.

Fortunately, he already had a plan. Reverse engineering a building wasn't hard. The answer had been obvious as soon as he talked with Dr. Terry.

"You'll find the deliverables are vague," Micah said, "but that's because I'm interested in any information about the tower's rapid construction. Whoever takes credit for this could too easily poach my company's investors, my best engineers, and my reputation. Help me be the first to learn the builder's secrets, and I'll happily write you that check."

"How about blueprints?" Chris offered. He bit his tongue. He shouldn't have given away the game.

"Bullshit," said Leon. "You don't have those."

"I know where to find them."

Micah smiled. "Call us when you do."

Chris went back outside.

The new cold front slipped inside the collar and sleeves of his winter coat. He looked up at the skyscraper. It didn't belong in this part of town, surrounded by houses and grassy lots. It didn't belong here at all, not popping up overnight like this.

But Eddie was in there. So Chris was going in, too.

And while inside, he'd grab that $200,000 reward.

He was continually stunned at executive blindspots. Dr. Terry had designed multi-million dollar buildings. Micah Rayner was the world's only hybrid tech/construction billionaire. But they'd never worked closely with general contractors or construction managers. Pompous elites like them always used middlemen to manage the folks who actually got their hands dirty. They'd never been the boots on the ground, making sure the building got built to plans.

If they had, they'd know that standard practice was to store the blueprints in the building's maintenance room, usually right on ground level.

Chris got in his car, ready to go make the easiest $200,000 of his life.

Leon came running out of the Steelside Cafe, waving to stop him.

11

———

CHRIS PUT the car back into park.

Leon pulled his camouflage coat tight around him against the biting wind. "Hold on a sec." He jogged to Chris's window.

Chris looked up at the bearded man. The skyscraper loomed behind him.

Chris felt his molars scraping together. "Did Micah change her mind?"

"What? No. You're still going after the blueprints. Micah, Roberts, and Dr. Terry are doing Dr. Terry's idea of admiring the design, or something like that. I'm going with you."

Chris shook his head. "So you can take the whole contract fee? Or half of it, when I'm the one with the plan?"

"Take a breath, why don't you? Fill your lungs with this cool air, and calm down a second. I already signed a contract with Micah. I'm on the clock. She thinks your plan is just as strong as Dr. Terry's—even though you were all mysterious about it—so I'm here to help you out. The open contract is still all yours. You mind if I ride with you? I just gotta grab something from my truck."

Leon jogged off before Chris could respond.

He didn't know if he could trust Micah. Leon seemed likable enough, but that was easily faked.

But he did trust written contracts. He stuck the paper inside the glovebox and locked it.

A second later, his back door opened. Leon threw a duffle bag on top of Chris's Home Depot purchases. Metal clanged against metal. The car jostled on its shocks.

Leon sat in the front seat. "You know the way?"

Chris looked at the skyscraper that filled up half the sky above them. "I can find it."

He drove down Hermitage, over I-95, and back into Richmond's Northside neighborhoods.

"How'd Micah find you?" Chris asked.

"College. We both went to Tech."

"Micah went to Tech?"

Leon laughed. "What, you don't think the Hokies could produce a billionaire? Micah was already in business—then she decided she needed a structural engineering degree and went back to school."

"And then she hired you?"

"Just for this job. We didn't keep in touch or nothing. She sent Roberts to offer me the gig at seven this morning."

"What do you usually do for work?"

"Building inspector out in Goochland."

"So Micah wanted a building inspector she could trust?"

"Eh, maybe that was part of it. Back in college, I liked to... explore... buildings. All the back corridors and service hallways."

"You're a building hacker?"

"I prefer 'urban explorer.' But I'm a little rusty now. It's been a solid ten years since I crawled through any ductwork."

"Why?"

"Because I'm forty! I've got kids."

"I mean, why crawl through ductwork?"

"It was exciting. And it made for good stories. I knew the whole Virginia Tech campus inside and out. Mostly inside, I guess. Then I got my first job in Chicago, and damn that was a good time. You know there's a panic room on each floor of the Sears Tower?"

"I'd never considered it."

"So anyways, that's why Micah sent me with you. They'll be admiring columns or some nonsense. Sounds like you'll actually be looking for something. I can help you get places."

That could be useful. But once Chris found Eddie, he was just after the maintenance room. He'd force an exterior door, then search the first floor. Maybe the basement. Find the maintenance room—also forcing that door if necessary—and then find the blueprints. If they were digital, he'd download them onto a thumb drive or just steal the whole computer.

"What about you? What's your secret talent? Why'd Micah want you?"

"I have no idea. I worked with Dr. Terry once. He admires my ability concerning office tasks."

"Is that what he said?"

"In his recommendation letters to architectural firms, yes."

"Shit. I knew I didn't like him." Leon leaned forward to peer up through the windshield. "What about your thesis? Micah mentioned it to Roberts."

Chris clenched his jaw. So they'd discussed how crazy Chris was before deciding it was okay to hire him.

"Did I find a sore spot?" Leon asked.

"It's fine. My thesis was a review of other academic papers."

"Oh. What were those about?"

"Misdating historical buildings. I got pretty caught up in theories saying that most of Christopher Wren's churches in London were ripoffs of Pict structures in northern Scotland, or that the Flat Iron building wasn't the first steel skyscraper. It was actually following a design in a small city in Vietnam."

"Why Vietnam?"

"That's where the paper I read said it happened. But it was fake. I was an excited kid, thinking I was piecing mysteries together. I didn't find out until later that the authors of the papers in my survey were either disgraced or lost their jobs, or in one case, they ended up in the looney bin."

"Maybe that's it."

"We're headed to the looney bin?"

"No, maybe that paper is why Micah hired you. Maybe she thinks this type of overnight construction has been done before."

"Even if my thesis was legit, knowing about other misdated buildings wouldn't help me understand how this tower appeared overnight. Besides, my thesis was why Dr. Terry screwed me out of credit on our project together. He said I embarrassed the college and didn't want my name anywhere next to his. That thesis is the opposite of a reason to hire me."

Leon shrugged. "Gotta be some reason."

"Dr. Terry thought I'd still be an overeager gofer."

"Sounded to me like Micah knew who you were before

Dr. Terry brought it up. But I could be wrong." Leon shrugged. "Who cares, we still get to explore an insane building. And we still get paid."

"After we find my son."

"Sure," Leon said. "Your son, who's about to be $200,000 richer."

Chris liked Leon's confidence. It made up for the anxiety that pumped through Chris as they drove closer, and the tower grew larger to block out more of the sky.

12

THE DRIVE from Lakeside back to the new building's Northside neighborhood took them from middle-class to lower-class homes.

Not the worst part of Richmond, but you wouldn't leave your car unlocked. A few of Chris's high school friends lived around here, and on social media he saw them occasionally complain about break-ins.

They followed the building to Barton Heights.

Earlier, Chris had rushed through here to catch Eddie and had barely noticed the city around him.

Now that Chris had a specific goal, the tools to do it, and a solid chance of walking away with $198,000 more than he'd ever had in his bank account, he could pay more attention to his surroundings.

Where Lakeside was quaint one-stories or cape cods, Barton Heights was largely Victorian design. High ceilings, tall windows, half-turrets. Not the sprawling mansions like houses built in the actual Victorian era, but a cheaper Victorian revival in Richmond during the roaring twenties.

But then a combination of white flight and the construction of I-95 had changed the economic demographics of the neighborhood.

Chris drove through the grid of houses.

He turned the corner past the Good Shepherd Church, a midcentury brick building that didn't fit the neighborhood, and then saw the tower in its entirety.

From a block away, the skyscraper blocked most of the sky. Smooth glass windows reflected gray clouds. A grid of narrow steel beams divided the windows unevenly. Chris couldn't get a sense of where one floor ended and the next began.

Only the first floor was obvious because it had the front doors.

Above that, the tiers appeared to be about ten floors each. Each tier was off-kilter to the one below it like a great hand had reached down from the sky and twisted it like a lightbulb.

They drove past Victorian homes toward the tower's cement steps. Chris looked more closely this time. The building had eight front doors, all the same reflective glass as the windows. Although these doors were a standard size, unlike the chaotic pattern of reflective windows that made up the rest of the building's faces.

There were square holes on the cement stoop, which Chris judged to be for dirt, mulch, and landscaping that hadn't yet been installed.

"Circle the building," Leon said. "Let's find the best way in."

On the next face of the building, it was flat and featureless. An empty cement canal waiting for landscaping looked like a medieval moat.

The far side of the building had eight doors, much like the front. Or maybe this was the front. Chris couldn't say it was identical because one window looked barely three feet high, while another looked over nine, but it was identical in absurdity.

The last face of the building was blank, like its opposite.

"The windows are ugly," Leon said.

"They must have taken forever to install," Chris said. "Different sizes like that, but no gaps? Custom sizes means nothing gets automated."

"It didn't take forever," Leon said. "It all happened last night. Unless you think there's some kind of trick."

Chris realized he hadn't sat back and thought about the possible explanations. His morning had been too busy, what with his life getting turned upside down.

"It's not a trick," Chris parked the car in front of a two-story white house with rotting siding. "Does that building look fake to you?"

"But how'd they do it?"

Chris shrugged. "They built it in pieces somewhere else, then stacked them on top of each other last night. That would explain the crooked construction."

"What if they built it underground and had like a giant elevator raise it up last night?" Leon suggested.

"I mean, it's impossible, but no more impossible than any other explanation."

"What do you think you'll find on the blueprints? Those'll be drawings of what it is, not how it got here."

"It'll have more than just a sketch. Materials, tolerances, phases."

"How many phases do you think they squeezed in last night?" Leon laughed. "Maybe you should have taken the first offer. There's nothing normal about this building; I'm wondering if the blueprints will be where you're thinking."

"As long as we find my son, I'll be fine," Chris said. "But the blueprints will be there, along with plenty of other info. There'll be some kind of answer in there. Let's go." He couldn't leave himself time to doubt. He'd start spiraling around his worry, giving it more life until it was all he could think about.

Chris got out of the car, ready to find answers.

13

———

CHRIS OPENED his Home Depot purchases and organized them in his backpack. The four-foot prybar he carried by hand.

Leon put on a vest covered in pockets, which he filled with various tools from his duffel bag. Handheld cameras, screwdrivers, glass cutters, and a collection of electrical tools Chris wasn't familiar with.

They walked to the cement stoops.

Chris looked around. They'd attracted a few onlookers, folks from Barton Heights who weren't working or at school. An old man on his porch. A mom putting a baby into a carseat.

"Think they'll call the cops?" asked Leon.

"Maybe. We'll be done by the time they get here." Chris stopped. "The better question is why the cops aren't here already. Or the news. Or the EPA. Isn't this weird enough for all that?"

"I'm sure they're coming. It's working its way through the bureaucrats to someone who can actually do something."

"What about the news?"

Leon shook his head. "Couldn't tell you."

"Let's ask someone." Chris jogged over to the young mom. His backpack clanked.

She shut the car door as he ran up, putting herself between Chris and her baby. Hastily brushed hair fell in front of her eyes. She wore khakis and a red department store polo with a name tag. *Tiffany.* "What do you want?" Tiffany asked.

Chris pointed behind him. "Did you see that building go up?"

She rubbed her arms in the cold. "Who are you? Cops?"

"I'm an architect. Just looking for a clue as to how that thing got built."

Tiffany relaxed. A little. "Like I told the other guy, it won't nothing but a dirt lot last night. I worked swing shift, got home at midnight. I looked straight across the empty dirt and noticed one of Mr. King's porch lights was burnt out. Then at five o'clock this morning, when the baby wanted a bottle, that ugly thing was reflecting my own porch lights back at me."

That narrowed the construction window even more. Sometime between midnight and five.

"Did they make noise putting it up?"

"Not a peep that I heard. My baby's a light sleeper. He would have been screaming if they did."

"You didn't see any construction equipment? Cranes? Trucks?"

"Nothing."

"And that didn't strike you as odd?"

"Of course it did! But I got a baby to take care of."

Chris understood that. Some things were more important

than others. But in his case, there was overlap. "Anybody on the street see anything that you know of?"

"I'm running on fumes. Taking the baby to my sister's so I can go to my second job. Only time I talk to my neighbors is when my days off line up."

"You said 'like you told the other guy,'" said Chris. "Who was that?"

Leon caught up. "Probably Micah's lawyer, or whatever investigators they hired."

"Could be," said the woman, "they didn't look like lawyers, though."

"The same folks who looked into the permits already knocked doors and took statements," Leon told Chris. "Nobody knows anything."

"No, these fellows were asking about a way inside. They didn't look all cleaned up like you two."

Chris didn't think Leon's camo coat and unkempt chest-length beard looked cleaned up, and neither did his own clothes. But he imagined a lawyer would look better.

"Must have been private investigators," said Leon. "Come on."

Chris thanked the young mom. He looked around again. The old man on his porch had gone back inside. He decided to take Leon's word that the neighbors would give the same answer. Nobody had seen anything, but the window for possible construction had shrunk even more. The tower had become a little more impossible.

He checked his phone for text messages. Nothing. He really wanted to get Eddie out of there.

"Alright," Chris said, "let's get the doors open."

14

———

THE DOORS WERE STILL LOCKED.

"Hold that prybar in the groove." Leon hefted a claw hammer. "I'll give it a few whacks."

The impact jarred Chris's hands, but the hammer blows forced the prybar between the steel door and its frame. The glass front cracked.

"Wedge it in closer to the lock itself," Leon said.

Chris followed his orders.

Another three hammer blows, a strong shove on the bar itself, and the lock snapped.

A brusque voice from behind surprised them both.

"What're you fellas doing?"

Chris jerked around.

At first, Chris thought it was Roberts. But this man was taller, at least six-foot-six, and his gut poked out more than Micah's bodyguard consultant. He had red hair, buzzed short. He chewed on an unlit cigarillo. Grape flavored tobacco drifted to Chris's nostrils.

The giant didn't have the same bulk as Roberts, but he

had lean, usable muscles. Dirt-stained fingertips and sun-leathered skin said this man worked outside with his hands.

"That's private property." He had a drawl that marked him from Chester or Petersburg, south of Richmond.

"You the owner?" Chris asked, knowing the answer.

"Boss asked me to keep folks out."

Leon wiped his nose. "Who's your boss? The owner?"

The man hesitated long enough to make it clear he was lying. "Yes."

"You sure you're not the grunt employee of someone who's going after Micah Rayner's open contract? Maybe trying to keep us from going after it ourselves?"

The man smiled, revealing yellowed teeth. His eyes flashed threatening glee. Chris stepped back into the glass door. It rattled on its busted hinges.

"What makes you think that?"

"If you worked for the owner, you'd call the police on us. But you're acting all tough by yourself."

"You scared?"

It was a schoolyard taunt, but the man was nearly a foot taller than Chris. He couldn't hope to match him physically.

"We're working directly for Miss Rayner," Leon said. "Your boss won't get shit if she disqualifies his eligibility for the open contract."

The buzzed redhead tilted his head like a confused dog. "Look, all I know is that you're not going in there. We need that contract to stay afloat. My boss owes me a month of backpay, and this is how he's getting it."

At the mention of money, Chris's fear of the man shrank beside his need to keep Eddie secure. He wielded the prybar with two hands. "Leon, did we get the door open?"

Leon yanked at the handle. Something cracked, and the door swung open. Humid warmth floated out into the chill morning.

Chris kept his eyes on the redhead, who smirked at the prybar.

"You ain't gonna stop me with that thing." He reached for it.

Chris drove the rounded end into his ample gut. He grunted, but the fat protected him from the brunt of the impact. He snarled at Chris.

Leon kicked him in the groin.

The man exhaled past puffed cheeks.

Chris ran through the open door into the building. Leon followed, dragging their bags. They yanked the door closed.

The lock wouldn't latch, so Chris stuck the prybar through the handle, and through the handle of the next door.

Still doubled over, the redhead yanked on the door from the outside, but the iron prybar held it firm. "I'll kick both your asses!" His voice was muffled through the glass.

After a minute, he gave up and pulled out his cell phone.

Chris and Leon turned around to inspect their sanctuary.

15

———

They walked through a claustrophobic foyer.

Low, tiled drop ceilings. A wide vestibule, nearly as wide as the block the building sat on. But shallow. Across from each exterior door, twenty feet away, were solid doors with small rectangular windows at the top.

Bright light shone through.

The outer doors rattled again. The redhead cupped his hands against the glass. His mouth moved like he was yelling. Chris didn't hear a thing, despite only a few moments ago hearing his muffled threats. The outer doors somehow were now completely soundproof, despite the busted latches and the doors only being held closed by the prybar. He could see daylight between the door and the jam, but sound wasn't getting through.

"We can't go back out that way," Chris said.

"Or any way, until he's gone," Leon said. "He'd see us going to your car."

"Maybe he'll be gone by the time we find what we're after," Chris said. But he felt trapped just the same.

He turned back around. "What we really need to worry about is that guy's boss. If he's half as unhinged as his friend out there, I don't want him around my son. Plus, if he's a general contractor, he might know where to look for the blueprints. I want to find the maintenance rooms before..."

Chris heard himself trail off. He was drawn to the inner doors. Through the small windows, he saw pieces of an inner courtyard, lit by sunlight, which didn't make sense—the outside of the building was all reflective glass.

He walked towards the light. Eddie would enjoy this. His trauma from his birth parents hadn't fully quashed his inquisitiveness. Chris saw his son creeping to the doors to press his face against their warm glass. Eddie pushed his shaggy brown hair out of his eyes and chewed on his thumbnail. He glanced over his shoulder.

"Eddie, wait for me." Chris reached for his boy.

"What's that?" Leon called from the far end of the dark foyer.

Chris blinked, looked around.

He'd gotten lost in his head, started speaking out loud as if his daydreams were real. Not the first time. Although, Eddie hadn't felt like a daydream.

Leon wasn't paying attention. He'd pulled out a compact telescoping ladder and was peering into a vent at the top of the wall.

Roberts, or the redhead rattling the doors and yelling at them, would have been able to stand on their toes and peer into the vent, the tops of their heads brushing the popcorn tile ceiling. Leon's small frame needed the ladder.

"Did you say something?" he called again.

Chris spared a look at the brightness through the inner

doors, shook his head to clear away lingering doubts about what he'd seen, then joined Leon. "Come on, let's check out the foyer."

"One sec. I'm just checking how difficult it'd be to get inside the vents."

"Looks like your shoulders would slide right in," Chris said. "You could fit two of you in there."

Leon laughed, deep, from his belly. "If I could get the cover off. You ever see screw heads like these?"

Chris leaned in. The screws holding on the vent cover were black, their heads at least half an inch in diameter. A head that wide was designed to spread its clamping pressure over a wide area, so it wouldn't break through anything when holding back high forces. "Why's it so big?"

"The cover itself doesn't weigh much. But you'd have a hell of a time trying to kick that out from the inside." Leon shrugged. "And look at this."

He shone his penlight on the screwhead. Instead of a flat slot, or a Philips head cross, it had four indented slits, forming a square.

"Looks like you'd unscrew it with two mini electrical plugs," Chris suggested.

"Did you bring any?"

"Must have forgot. Where do you even buy a screw like that?"

"Fabricate it yourself," Leon said. "But I'm more interested in the screwdriver that fits this. Look how tiny the slots are. You'd snap apart your tool trying to loosen this unless it was cut from a solid piece of steel. Somebody's carrying around a four-pronged screw driver with needle-thin prongs that won't snap. What's that tell you about how they built this tower?"

"Custom machined parts can be tracked down. Can't be but so many shops that can output the thousands of screws they'd need just for the vent covers."

Leon de-telescoped his ladder, stuffed it in his duffle bag, and threw the bag over his shoulder. "I guess. But custom materials would slow a project down. They built this overnight, remember."

That was looking more impossible by the second. They were standing on tile floors. Tile glue took twenty-four hours to set. The walls were drywall. Drywall mud took just as long to dry. And these walls were painted. The foyer didn't smell of fresh paint. It smelled more like cinnamon air freshener.

"Damn this is wild." Leon's white smile reflected the bright light from the inner doors. "I haven't been this excited since my brakes jammed on my four-wheeler last summer. Try steering through downhill switchbacks with your back wheels stuck solid." He laughed. "Let's find this maintenance room of yours. Maybe they'll have some driver bits that fit those vent screws."

"First we find my son." Chris looked back at his prybar, still holding the door closed.

The redhead now stood back from the doors, yelling into a phone and leaning backwards to look up at the building. The impossibly soundproofed doors kept him silent.

Chris wanted his prybar. Redhead's boss would likely be just as willing to commit violence for money.

"Hold on," Chris said to Leon. He jogged softly to the outer doors. He lifted his prybar off the handles, and gently slid it free. The doors stayed silent.

The latches and hinges were solid. The crack they'd put in the glass was gone.

Maybe the crack was only in the outer pane, and he couldn't see it from inside. But that wouldn't explain the latching mechanism fixing itself. They'd snapped it in half.

"What are you doing?" Leon hissed.

The redhead glanced their way.

Chris froze.

He went back to yelling at the phone. He hadn't seen them. The doors were opaque from the outside.

Chris gently pushed on the door they'd broken. It held closed.

He thought up a dozen explanations. None of them held water.

He must have been wrong about breaking the latch.

But he couldn't spend time solving this mystery. The only mystery that mattered right now was which direction Eddie went. Then after that, the money for Eddie's solid home.

They headed through the inner doors.

16

―――――

CHRIS EXPECTED A BLAND FOYER. Instead, he found an open courtyard.

It felt so welcoming that he felt slighted when Leon didn't slow down to appreciate it.

Chris spread his arms, opening to embrace his surroundings.

The ceiling was thirty stories above. Office windows lined two of the walls, random in size and placement. The other two walls were the outer glass of the skyscraper. Four bridges crossed the open space, the first only three floors above.

The courtyard itself was open, airy, and comforting. Directly across from the doors they'd come in were another set of identical doors. To either side were sand-colored elevator doors, and beyond those were doors to stairwells.

The center of the courtyard was a tiled floor, and in a checkerboard pattern across the floor were square planters with knee-high grass that tilted and shuddered in a shifting breeze.

Bright sunlight warmed the courtyard. The glass of the

windows themselves must have been coloring the light, because the cold November sun outside was filtered through gray clouds, and left the outside world in dull, cool colors. But inside, the light warmly colored the bright green grass and tile the color of beach sand.

To their left, there was a round structure with a lobby desk in front of it. The building management's offices would be in that wood igloo.

To their right, the checkerboard planters grew shorter until the waving grass's sod was level with the floor itself. A pond as big as a basketball court filled that end of the court-yard. The pond had no retaining walls, so gentle waves lapped at the grass and tile.

Chris imagined setting a beach chair by the pond, leaning back, then staring at the open space above until his heart slowed and his problems melted into little frustrations he could solve with a snap of his fingers.

Leon stomped to the center of the courtyard.

"Slow down," Chris said. He followed Leon. The breeze that massaged the grass felt cool on Chris's cheeks. It smelled of fresh dandelions.

"A second ago you were in a hurry." Leon hesitated in the middle of the courtyard. He looked from the wooden igloo to the elevator. "Where'd you say the maintenance room is? Back in the hut, or down in the basement?"

Chris grew distracted by the pond. The glass behind it was frosted, so he couldn't see through to the neighborhood outside. But the closer he looked, the more the pond's reflec-tion stretched into a horizon of gentle waves. The light fixture's reflection even looked like a sunrise.

Maybe everything would work out.

The absurdity of the thought shattered his calm. Sherri was gone. Things would only "work out" once he had the income to give Eddie a stable home.

He shook his head. Eddie was in here somewhere. That was the most pressing issue.

Chris refocused.

Leon snapped his fingers in Chris's face. "Don't slow down or you'll start thinking of your ex wife."

"Technically not my ex, yet."

"Trust me, you don't want to try to win her back. I've been there. She kicked you in the balls. The best remedy is a shooting range. Two handguns at one time. You don't hit a thing, but it feels amazing. Of course, they tear up your membership card after that."

"You lost me."

"I'm saying let's keep moving. Are we going in there?" He pointed to the wooden igloo behind the reception desk. "Or down there?" He pointed to a stairwell door next to the elevator.

"Uh," Chris felt like he'd just woken up from a nap or finished a deep tissue massage. His muscles felt relaxed, his vision soft. He didn't understand why Leon wasn't getting the same effect from this courtyard. "My son, first."

"Where do you think he went? You said he's looking for treasure."

Chris turned his back on the pond. His thoughts grew sharper. He checked his phone once more. No service. Where would Eddie have gone?

If he was living out their treasure hunting video game, then the level with the skyscraper had gold coins stashed all throughout. The biggest stash moved with each playthrough.

But when Chris and Eddie played together, they always checked the basement first.

"We should head downstairs. But let's check in there first." He pointed to the wood igloo. If the blueprints were in such an obvious place, he couldn't put off searching for them. Another contractor might grab them first. Two minutes wouldn't put Eddie in anymore trouble.

"Lead the way," Leon said.

Chris cinched up his backpack, adjusted his grip on the prybar, and headed for the reception desk.

Someone shouted down at them from above.

17

"Up here!"

A gravely voice. A man leaned over the railing of the highest skybridge.

Chris's stomach flipped at the risk of it. If he slipped, it was thirty stories down to land on the cold tile floor.

Leon craned his neck to peer up. "Think that's redhead's boss?"

"Must be," Chris said.

"Ain't nothing you want down there!" shouted the man. "Take the elevator. It's rejuvenating. Or the stairs too. More direct!"

Chris's heart sunk. They'd been beaten to the prize.

"He's drunk," Leon said.

Chris shouted up to him. "What'd you find?" He wanted to ask about Eddie, but if the man hadn't run across him, Chris didn't want to give him any ideas.

"Come and see!"

"If he's giving away the farm," Leon said, "you'd be a fool not to take it."

"He can't be. Not if he set a guard to keep us out."

"Unless he drank too many breakfast beers. Maybe he's a generous drunk."

Chris looked over at the pond. Just the glance relaxed his shoulders, slowed his breathing. He shook his head. "Something weird about it."

"You mean this guy giving away information that could be worth 200k? I'm telling you, he's on drugs. Let's go up and take advantage."

The breeze picked up. It was softly warm, a comforting feeling after being outside. The pond lapped more loudly at the tile floor.

"No," Chris said.

The air stilled. The pond quieted.

"Let me show you!" called the man from above.

"If he's found something, he's found it," Chris said. "That's not my top priority anyways."

Still, he led the way to the wooden igloo.

18

THEY WALKED behind the reception desk and through the igloo doorway.

Chris paused to let his eyes adjust.

The breeze of the courtyard whistled past the igloo's windows. Light shone through the windows and from globe light fixtures.

Half-circles of desks lined either wall. Atop each desk sat a telephone, a pen, and a pad of paper—twelve workstations in all.

Leon flipped through one pad, then picked a phone up off the hook to listen to it. "Dead. You think this is going to be a call center? Operator station for the building?"

"Twelve operators?" Chris tested one of the pens—it worked—then pocketed it.

"Hey, check this out," Leon said. He'd opened a desk drawer and pulled out a laminated brochure.

Chris found an identical one in another desk.

It read "Directory" across the top.

A surge of hope flashed inside Chris. It quickly died.

Below the headline was a list of numbers without descriptions.

Starting at B3, counting down to B1, then up from 1 to 120.

Leon tossed his aside. "What kind of directory just has floors? Shouldn't it be office suites?"

"There aren't a hundred-twenty floors in here," said Chris. "From outside it looked like around sixty."

"Let's go see what the elevator says," Leon suggested.

"Hold on." Chris opened the rest of the desk drawers, but found only 12 copies of the useless directory. Nothing else in the room. "Okay, let's go."

They'd wasted less than a minute, but come up empty-handed. Time to search the basement.

They walked across the courtyard to the elevators. Chris pressed the down arrow button.

A bell dinged, a light above the doors switched on, and the doors slid open.

They stepped inside. Chris kept his hand on the door to hold it open.

"There you go." Leon pointed to the wall of buttons. "One hundred and twenty, plus the three sub levels."

Chris poked his head out of the elevator and looked up. Around thirty open floors. Four bridges across the open space. The ceiling was a smooth surface, probably plastic with a textured paint.

He stopped to remind himself there was no way that could have been constructed in one night.

"You can't see all hundred and twenty floors from in here," Leon said.

"I didn't see that many outside, did you? I was guessing 60. Maybe 70."

Leon shrugged. "I didn't count. We could go to the top, see how high it is."

"No, let's search the basement first. That's where my son would look for treasure first. And it's my best guess for finding the blueprints."

"Fine by me." Leon pressed the button B3.

"Wait, let's take the stairs." But the door was already shutting. Chris tried to hold back the door. It didn't give. He pulled his hand away before it was crushed. He mashed the open doors button. No response. "I guess we're taking the elevator."

Somewhere below, a motor kicked to life. The floor juddered, and they descended.

19

———————

THE SCREEN above the door displayed a red LED "B1," then "B2," then "B3."

The elevator stopped. The motor below them stopped humming. Its last breath echoed deep beneath.

Chris pressed the open doors button.

"What if they built it underground," Leon suggested, "and they raised it overnight?"

"The neighbors would have noticed the sixty-story pit. Or a hundred and twenty-story. Whichever."

"Unless it just looked normal up top. They kept the top layer of dirt."

"Aren't you a structural engineer? I'm sure you could name a thousand reasons that wouldn't work."

Leon shrugged. "I'm just thinking. We're in the bottom subbasement. But..." He stomped his foot. The noise echoed beneath them, repeating increasingly softly as the sound waves fell away. "That's some empty space down there."

This whole thing was getting out of control.

But he had to admit, the strangeness of this building was a fantastic distraction from the disaster this morning.

Chris only needed a simple answer. Or something that could lead Micah to an answer. So far, he'd only found more proof that the impossible building was impossible. Now he had another mystery.

"It could be your answer," Leon said.

"*My* answer? What about you?"

"I'm getting my paycheck either way. I'm having fun."

Chris tapped the prybar on the floor. Again, the echo repeated and then faded. If they found an empty space beneath the building, that would be an answer for Micah. "Alright, after we look for my boy, we'll see if the maintenance room is down here and see if there's a lower subbasement. Maybe a different elevator."

"Sounds like a plan," Leon said. He pressed the open doors button.

The doors didn't respond.

Chris's heartbeat picked up. He didn't wait for claustrophobia to set in. He jammed the prybar in between the doors and wriggled it until he found purchase, then pulled hard.

"Whoa," Leon said.

Chris's shoulders strained, and the doors creaked open. Light from the elevator spilled into the darkness beyond.

A concrete floor. Exposed ceiling with pipes and conduit.

"Hope you brought a flashlight," Leon said.

Chris rummaged through his backpack for the flashlight he'd bought. He put batteries inside, and switched it on.

The hallway outside the elevator was cramped. Pipes and conduit lined the walls as well as the ceiling. They narrowed the hallway even more with jagged geometric patterns.

Chris couldn't imagine Eddie exploring down here by himself. He was strong-willed, but he was still nine.

Leon switched on his own lights, a headlamp and a heavy police baton flashlight. He whistled. "It's gorgeous. Used to be, if I could find a hallway like this, it would take me anywhere in the building. Or at least the surrounding floors." He stepped through the elevator doors.

Chris followed. Leon's attitude bothered him. The courtyard had been relaxing and happy. There was some architectural psychology going on up there with the open air and the simulated beach. Sub level 3 wasn't quite that feeling's opposite—moreso its absence. There were no architectural decisions made down here. Pipes, ducts, and wire conduit took their own paths.

If they ever found the designers, Chris felt confident the designer of the courtyard would be someone he followed on Twitter, and the designer of the sub levels would be an engineer.

Leon shone his lights around the elevator door. It took up the entire end of the narrow hallway. "No stairwell," Leon said. "Let's send the elevator back up and keep the doors wedged open. Get a look at how far down the shaft goes."

"Hell, no. Not until we find the stairs."

"Chicken?"

"Call me what you want, I'm not getting stuck down here." Chris would bet dollars to donuts that Eddie came down here, got spooked, and headed back upstairs to search the next hiding spot in their video game. But there was still a chance. "Let's explore a bit. Find the maintenance room."

They walked down the hallway, shoes tapping on the concrete floor. Chris stayed in the middle of the walkway, trying not to think about being buried alive. The air was still and dry. Their flashlights lit up thirty feet of hallway as bright as upstairs, and another thirty feet in gray shadow.

Chris called Eddie's name. It echoed dully.

"If your boy is wandering around down here," Leon said, "then he could be a killer building hacker one day."

"One thing at a time." Chris adjusted his backpack straps.

Leon peered behind conduits and ducts. "No closets, no nothing. What's on the other side of these walls?"

"Probably dirt."

A low chugging of HVAC equipment grew louder as they walked. They reached a crossroads. The same hallway in four directions.

Chris called for Eddie again. Thick echoes from each hallway. No response.

"He's not down here," Leon said. "Let's check out the maintenance room. My money says it's nearby all that racket."

They went towards the HVAC noise.

After three minutes of walking, Leon asked, "Are we still under the building? I think we've walked too far."

"Probably just feels that way because it's so claustrophobic in here."

"What do you mean? It's like a warm blanket. Cozy."

Finally, the tone of the HVAC noise changed. It was no longer muffled by a wall. Ahead, they found an open doorway. Inside, their flashlights illuminated a room of shuddering steel boxes the size of shipping containers. Chris assumed they were air handlers.

"I've never seen units like this," Leon said. "Of course, Goochland's pretty rural. The buildings I inspect wouldn't need this much air."

"They don't connect to anything," Chris noticed. He banged on a duct in the hallway. "None of these pipes even go in here."

"Are they even air handlers?" Leon walked inside.

Chris shone his light either direction up the hallway. He couldn't explain why, but he felt the need to keep watch while Leon investigated.

"No, here we go." Leon crouched down to shine his light under the closest steel box. "There's pipes into the floor."

He stomped on the concrete. "Feels solid. I thought they'd only lay concrete slabs on the lowest floor, but those pipes go somewhere."

"Sewer?" Chris suggested.

"Wrong kind of pipe," Leon said. "I'm telling you, we're on top of a big pit where they lifted the building out of."

Chris leaned into the room to check for any other doorways. Sometimes the maintenance room was attached to the HVAC room. He couldn't see any of the far walls with the steel boxes in the way. He took a step inside, but saw movement down the hallway in his peripheral vision. He whipped his flashlight around.

"Eddie?" Back the way they'd come, Chris thought he saw a shady figure walking away out of the furthest, gray reaches of his light. "Walking" wasn't the right word, though. He couldn't make out limbs, only the blurriest figure, but it was too tall to be Eddie.

It moved in quick lurches, up and forward and down, up and forward and gone.

Chris held his breath. His skin crawled. The stillness of the basement air felt thick. He stretched, holding the flashlight as far out as he could without stepping away from the doorway and out of view of Leon. He saw only the cement and pipes of the hallway.

"What are you looking at?"

Leon's cheery question startled Chris.

Leon laughed. "Getting spooked by shadows?"

Chris shook his head, but kept his light trained down the hall. "Maybe. Or could be someone else after the bounty." He didn't like the idea of other contractors bumping into Eddie. And the more he thought about it, he didn't want Eddie in here at all. Apart from the obvious, something was right about this building.

"You're jumping at shadows," Leon said. "You were edging up to a panic attack as soon as we got down here. " But he came out and shined his flashlights, too.

"I saw someone."

Leon called out, "Hello?"

No echo. The pipes and conduit jutting out from the wall and ceilings in this corridor trapped the sound waves.

"See?" Leon said. "You hate basements. No biggie."

"I don't hang out in a lot of basements," Chris said, "but I've never hallucinated before."

"Not a hallucination. Just catching the shadow wrong when you're nervous. Big difference."

Nerves hadn't created that quick lurching. "Let's find the maintenance room and get back to the courtyard."

They kept on the direction they'd started. They quickly found the end of the hall: a simple wall with a closed blue door.

Chris readied the prybar.

Leon tried the handle. The door swung open.

20

CHRIS LEANED through the open doorway.

Opening the door had shifted the pressure in the air, and a soft breeze blew out of the room. Inside, his flashlight revealed a space no bigger than his kitchen at home. Steel cabinets lined the back wall. The other two walls were bare cement to match the floor.

"Awesome." Leon walked up to open the first cabinet. "Maybe we'll find some driver bits to fit those weird-ass screws in the vent covers."

"Wait." Chris didn't know why he said it.

Leon was already opening the cabinet. Hinges squeaked.

Chris flinched, ready to leap out into the hall.

"Nothing." Disappointment dripped from Leon's voice. He opened the cabinet wider. Empty shelves.

Chris noticed a pattern in the concrete floor. Waves and swirls from flattening and polishing, which together pointed toward a closed steel cabinet. That must have been where they started the polishing machine, when they did this room. He knew that didn't make sense, but nothing did.

Leon opened that cabinet to reveal a stack of short, wide drawers.

"Blueprints," Chris said. That style of cabinet decorated every architectural firm he'd been in. Wide enough to hold drawings.

"I figured they'd be on a computer."

"Me, too." Chris slid open the top drawer. The drawer slides glided smoothly and silently. Inside, a stack of thick off-white paper. He removed the top sheet. Leon shined his flashlights on it.

"Hot damn," whispered Leon. "You found it."

Black, blue, and green lines covered the paper. Black outlined the square of the building's outer walls and the hallways and rooms within it. Fixtures like stairways, doors, and windows were in blue.

"Looks like the basement we're in now."

Chris nodded. There was the elevator they'd come down, and the intersection where they'd turned down here. There was the room with the shuddering HVAC units.

Inside that room was the green ink. The strange symbols weren't any representation that Chris had ever seen on building blueprints. Each was about the size of a quarter, only most weren't round. They were triangular but with gaps in the sides, or inverted corners. Series of dots and dashes filled many of them. They weren't printed; they looked hand drawn. The thickness of the green lines varied with the weight the artist had put into his pen.

"What are those?" Leon asked.

Chris scratched at the green lines. It wasn't ink on top of the page. More like a laser printer. But that didn't make sense with the wavering thickness of the lines. They must have used a drawing program Chris wasn't familiar with. "Couldn't tell you. Something to do with those HVAC units that pipe into the floor."

"Should we take another look at them?"

Chris didn't want to hang around down here any longer than necessary. "Let's get these plans upstairs into better light, and see if there's any answers."

"Sure, but I still want to send an elevator up and look down the shaft. Looks like there's an elevator and stairs over this way." Leon pointed on the plan to the opposite end of the hallway where they now stood.

They removed the contents of twelve drawers and rolled up over a hundred sheets, into six thick rolls. They tied them off with zip-ties that Leon had in his bag.

"You take a lot of people hostage while you're building hacking?" Chris asked.

"Sometimes you want to make sure a door stays open behind you."

They headed back. Leon shined his light into the HVAC room while they passed, but Chris urged him on. He kept expecting the lurching figure to appear again.

They passed straight through the intersection from before.

"We turned right here before," Chris said.

"Yeah, so?"

"But now these plans say there's an elevator and stairs straight ahead."

"Don't back out on me now. I want to see what's down there."

"I'm saying, up on the ground floor, this supposed elevator and stairs would be in the pond."

"Huh. Could be behind the pond."

"It was windows straight to outside. No space."

"Then maybe it's just to the basement levels."

Not an exit, then. The thought of walking deeper into this cavern made the walls close in, and their footsteps sound deader.

Oh no. They'd only searched the lowest of three basements. Eddie could be on the other two. Chris wanted to get back into sunlight. Eddie was nine—he wouldn't spend any more time down here in the dark than he had too. He was probably upstairs already. If Chris remembered their video game correctly, the next possible hiding spot for the treasure would be on the sixth floor. But first he had to get out of this basement.

"Easy there, chief." Leon had noticed Chris breathing heavier. "I'll take a quick look, and then we'll head back upstairs."

Another three minutes of walking and they reached the end of the hallway. The narrow corridor opened twice as wide before shiny silver elevator doors, and a closed steel door with the right angles of a staircase etched onto it.

Chris shuffled the blueprints into the crook of his arm. He pressed the up button. A bell dinged. Motors churned below them.

"It was already up," Leon said. "We should have pried the doors first."

The hum of the elevator grew louder. Its tone grew deeper as it slowed. The bell dinged again, and the doors slid open.

Yellow light poured into the hallway. It emphasized the disjointedness of the pipes and ductwork more than the white light of their LED flashlights.

"Send it back up so we can peek and get out of here," Chris said. To help calm his nerves, he thought of the two hundred thousand dollars.

Leon handed his share of the blueprints to Chris and stepped inside.

"Hey, look at this," Leon said.

Chris's arms were full of three-foot rolls of paper. "What is it?"

"The elevator's not just the basement floors. Goes all the way up to one-twenty."

Chris mapped out the path they'd taken in his head. It matched what they'd seen on the blueprint. "That doesn't make sense. There was no elevator on this side of the lobby."

"We must have got turned around. I'll send it up." Leon press a button.

The doors starting sliding closed, faster than they'd opened.

Chris thrust his foot against one, but like before, they had no pressure sensor to stop them.

Leon slipped through, but his duffel bag caught on the doors. Chris dropped the blueprints to yank the strap off Leon's shoulder.

Leon fell out onto the concrete floor.

The doors closed with an audible clang. The yellow light of the elevator car disappeared.

"Shit, my gear." Leon jump back to his feet and mashed the up button.

Chris caught his breath. "That elevator was trying to cut you in half."

"Miscalibrated pressure sensor," Leon said. "That'd fail inspection, but it's an easy fix."

"Calibrated to not work at all," Chris said.

"Nah, just a screw-up. Let's get this door open."

"You already hit the button," Chris said. "The elevator will be back."

"I sent it up to one-twenty. We've got time."

Chris rolled the blueprints away from the elevator doors, then jimmied them open with his prybar. Their flashlights lit up the elevator shaft. Concrete walls with steel tracks to keep the elevator car stable. The cables hung taut in the middle of the open space.

Chris leaned in and shined his light upwards. The same view for at least thirty feet. Little lines of sunlight above where it leaked through doors above them. "It shouldn't be concrete. The building is steel. Why would the elevator shaft be concrete?"

Leon was leaning in, looking in the opposite direction. "Whoa boy. This goes down another six levels at least."

Chris looked down. The same view as above, only without the trickles of sunlight. Their flashlights didn't reach the bottom.

Leon whistled. "My theory about building underground and then raising it makes a lot more sense now, huh?"

Chris had to admit it was better than anything he'd come up with yet. Of course, he still had to inspect the plans.

"There weren't any buttons lower than B3 in the elevator," Leon said. "How do we get down there?"

The urge to flee up the staircase nearly overpowered Chris. There shouldn't be another six levels below them. They were already three stories below ground. This was a vacant lot yesterday. The pit loomed up at him, an inverse of the tower above. What if it was one hundred twenty floors up and the same number down? Over fifteen-hundred feet of hole beneath him. If he slipped, he'd have a solid twelve seconds to contemplate his death.

What if Eddie had slipped?

He took a deep breath. Stepped back from the open shaft.

There was no reason to think Eddie would be peeking beneath elevators. He was too small to pry open the doors, anyways.

Chris counted to ten.

If the building had been constructed underground, then there'd be some sort of lift. Finding that lift would satisfy Micah's contract, and Chris would have enough money to give Eddie a stable home.

This pit was a problem that could be solved.

"Let's try the stairwell." He opened the door. The stairwell was as dark as the basement hallways. His flashlight revealed the same concrete floor and an iron staircase. That was unorthodox, expensive, and a maintenance headache. Add it to the list of nonsensical construction decisions that made the foyer, basement, and stairwells seem like the product of a first-year architecture student—how an amateur assumed a skyscraper would be, without knowing any of the thousand restricting rules that came from practical construction and design.

But the key thing Chris noticed about the stairs was that they only went up. No way down to the emptiness below.

"There's gotta be some different stairs," Leon said. "Some way to get down there."

"If your theory is right, that this building was built under-ground and then raised up—which again, is impossible—then the whole thing was raised, including the basement levels. If this is the bottom floor, then it's empty space below us, except for whatever lifts raised the building. Whatever's now holding it up.

Leon nodded, thinking. "Telescoping elevator shafts."

"What?"

"Whoever built it needs some way to get down there to do maintenance on the lift. When the building raised up, the elevator shaft extended like a telescope. I bet the right key will allow us to descend below, like you'd need for a penthouse."

"We don't need to go down there-"

"The hell we don't. I want to see it."

"Okay, after we find my son, you can go spelunking." Even still, the building's mystery pulled at Chris. "But for Micah's contract, if this building was somehow raised on impossible hydraulic lifts, then we need evidence of those lifts. Or at least of the empty space below us. I bought an inspection camera. It'll only reach fifteen feet, but I've got some rope so we can lower the whole thing and record."

"I've got a thirty-foot endoscope camera in my bag."

"I'm not waiting for it."

Leon mashed the button a few more times. They both looked up the shaft. No movement. The cables were still.

"Let's go with what we have," Leon said.

They powered up Chris's inspection camera, a digital camera with the lens on the end of a stiff wire. Chris had bought it on impulse with Sherri's credit card. You never knew when you'd want to see under a door or around a corner.

The camera was normally used to see inside walls, but the distance would let them see what was below their feet. If

Leon's theory was right, and only the elevator shaft continued down—not the whole building—then there'd be no doors to block their view. Just a gap in the shaft where the floors used to be.

They tied up the camera, attached Leon's headlamp, lowered the endoscopic lens first, set it to record, and then lowered the rope. Chris lowered it slowly. He couldn't see what the camera was picking up, so he allowed it to gently rotate in his hands, and let it carefully slip downwards until he reached the end of his fifty-foot rope.

"Alright, bring it back up, just as slow," Leon said.

Chris glanced up to make sure the elevator wasn't coming back down. Nothing but tiny lines of sunlight. The cables in the center of the shaft were still.

He pulled the camera back up.

They stepped away from the open shaft to hunch over the display screen on the back of the camera. The camera hadn't lined up perfectly with the headlamp, so the video showed the washed-out circle of light off to one side. The view of the elevator shaft rotated and descended. Ten seconds into the video, Chris and Leon saw the first opening in the shaft below them. The camera panned past the empty square. Despite the headlamp's fifty-foot range, the darkness beyond the opening and below the basement floor swallowed the light completely. Another ten seconds into the video, another gap with the same results.

They saw four total empty doorways before the rope reached its limit.

"Looks empty," Leon said.

Chris had to agree. The concrete floor under his shoes suddenly felt fragile. "Now can we go back upstairs?"

Leon rewound the video at normal speed. "Did you see that?"

He repeated the moment that the camera passed the final door, four vacant levels below them. A pinprick of light reflected back. "When my iPad makes its way back down here, we can blow up that image. Could be the lift you're talking about."

Chris leaned in close to the camera's display screen. He replayed the tiny reflection. His stomach turned in knots. "Hold it still." He watched it again and couldn't deny what he was seeing. Whatever caught the light, it *lurched*.

21

———

CHRIS COULDN'T SCOOP up the blueprints fast enough.

Whoever he'd seen lurching down the basement hallway was now below them, in the empty space beneath the building.

This wasn't a construction mystery—it was something weirder.

And Eddie was still inside.

"What's the deal?" Leon squatted to pick up a stray blueprint. He lowered his flashlight, which cast shadows of angled conduit across the floor.

The walls seemed to move in closer, and the fragile concrete floor looked ready to crack and send them tumbling into the earth below.

"It's the same thing I saw outside the HVAC room." Chris lugged his armful of blueprints to the stairwell door.

"Just floating in the air down there? You're assuming a lot from a little dot of light."

"It moved the same," Chris said.

"The same as what?"

Chris realized he hadn't told Leon what he'd actually seen, only that he'd seen something. No, *somebody*. It had to be a person, hopping instead of walking. Chris shined his flashlight back down the hallway. Nothing. "Can we discuss this upstairs?"

"Sure, but if this fella is walking around down there, it means there's floors. Maybe there's another stairwell-"

"We'll look for it on the blueprints." Chris's prybar slipped and clanged to the floor.

Leon picked it up to hand it back. He led the way up the iron staircase.

Chris focused on keeping his balance between carrying four rolls of blueprints, his prybar, and aiming his flashlight at his feet.

The walls were blank, none of the usual exit signs or stencil-painted floor numbers.

Leon whistled. "These stairs are killer. I need to hit the gym."

Chris grunted. He wanted to look back, make sure that they weren't being followed. But he couldn't risk dropping the blueprints and having to go back down for them.

They rounded one landing. "That'll be sub-level two," Chris said. His thighs burned.

"I know urban exploration isn't everybody's thing." Leon's voice was farther ahead than Chris realized. "But I do think you gotta appreciate this experience. Life comes at you, and what can you do but pick a point and head for it?"

Chris hurried to keep up. "I don't need a shrink." He almost bumped into Leon.

Leon panted. "I know, my bad. That's some serious shit you're going through with your wife."

Chris's thighs screamed at him now to slow down the pace. He glanced over his shoulder but couldn't point the flashlight back without rearranging his grip on the blueprints. The stairs behind him were vague outlines. "My wife can jump off a bridge. I'm worried about getting out of this basement, finding my son, and getting the money to keep our home. In that order."

"Sure, sure," said Leon. He went silent for a moment, then said, "I really forgot how amazing this feels. After today, I'm getting back into this. I'll hack every building in Richmond, then go up to D.C. I could get back to being the best in the world. I'm destined for great things. That's a weird thing to say, isn't it?"

Chris laughed. "No kidding. What are you smoking?"

He shined his light up from his feet to the stairs above. The dull iron steps soaked in the light, but the white LED was enough to see up this flight and the next. Untouched gray walls enclosed this neglected artery. Chris squeezed the blueprints until they wrinkled.

He jerked around, pointing his light back the way he'd come. More of the same dull stairwell.

Leon was gone.

22

THE TOWER'S weight compressed the air of the stairwell. It draped heavy on Chris's shoulders, dripped thick down his throat.

"Leon?" he called.

No echo. The architecture snatched sound waves and clutched them tightly. Chris considered that maybe these outer spaces weren't designed by an amateur, but that they'd been designed for a purpose Chris hadn't yet considered: to isolate.

The flashlight and prybar grew slick in his sweaty grip. Every shuffling step sounded a sharp staccato.

He was alone, over a story beneath the earth.

He shined his light up to the next landing, between sub-basement levels one and two. No way Leon could have sprinted past there. Chris had just bumped into him.

Back the way they'd come was the same—the empty landing of sub basement two. Leon would have had to push past him.

Chris leaned over the railing. He couldn't imagine Leon

falling without making a noise. His flashlight beam didn't reach the concrete floor of sub-basement level three. That wasn't right. The bottom should be only three landings down. Chris counted. Five, before the light couldn't reach anymore.

"No," he whispered. He couldn't look away from the depths of the hollow stairwell. It was impossible. Three minutes ago, there'd been a solid floor. He thought of Leon falling, flailing, tensed for an impact that never came.

"That didn't happen," Chris told the darkness. "I would have seen his flashlights thrashing around."

Then where was he?

Chris inspected the wall but found only smooth concrete. The steps didn't even rattle under Chris's heavy stomps.

"He must have switched off his lights and sprinted ahead." His voice hung dull, echoless. Chris bit his tongue. He didn't need to hear that again.

Nothing to do but head up. Maybe Leon would be waiting for him in the courtyard.

A soft thud on a step far below.

Chris leaned over the railing once again.

The noise repeated.

He jerked his flashlight across the gap, along the sides, everywhere below.

Louder. Closer.

A thud, then a quick dragging. Like shoving a kitchen table across a linoleum floor.

Chris climbed to the next landing, still balancing the blueprints and pointing his flashlight down. He couldn't spot the source of the noise.

A mental image of the sound clicked into place. The *drag, thud, drag* played in time to the lurching figure's movement.

Not thirty feet below him, come up from a staircase that didn't exist five minutes ago, the thing came for him.

Rational thought fled. Chris crushed his bundle against his chest and dashed up the stairs. He fell twice. The second time, after the closed door of subbasement one, he cut his shin open on the iron step.

As he turned the final corner, fear screamed in his head that the stairwell had stretched itself downward, and so it must have done the same upwards. There would be no courtyard door, only an eternity of basements, where he'd be chased by the lurcher until he took his own life by diving down the open maw in the center of the stairwell, falling, falling, until he caught up to Leon, whose starved corpse would break apart from the force of their eternal terminal velocity.

Sunlight.

Under the door on the next landing.

Chris yanked the door open to barge into the blinding glow.

23

───────

HE LET the blueprints and his prybar fall to the tile floor.

Chris staggered away from the stairwell door, which shut firmly behind him. It was next to the elevator he and Leon had gone down. They'd been more turned around down there than he realized.

The sun through the windows above the pond warmed his face. He squinted from the brightness.

The stairwell should have taken him up through the pond, but somehow he'd ended up right where they'd started. If he'd taken that same elevator back up instead, where would he have ended up?

He looked around, hopeful for Leon.

Instead, coming out of the wooden igloo into the checker-board pattern of grass planters were Roberts, Micah Rayner, and Dr. Terry.

"Did you see Leon come through here?" he asked.

Dr. Terry, who was last to emerge from the igloo, adjusted his thick glasses atop his bulbous nose. "Were you chasing him? Heavens, boy, you look like a wild man."

Chris couldn't spare the effort to care about Dr. Terry's pretentious barbs. Although he hoped Leon was okay for Leon's sake, the bigger issue was determining the danger inside this building. Something had chased him up those stairs. Leon had disappeared. How much danger was Eddie in?

Micah approached, arms crossed over her slender chest. Her expression was impossible to read. "I told Leon to stay with you. Where is he?"

"We were headed back upstairs, and something was behind us... no, that happened afterwards..." Chris tried to gather his thoughts, but all he could think of was that black maw inside the stairwell, reaching deep into the ground. He purposely bit his tongue. "We got separated."

Micah raised an eyebrow. Her stoic expression shifted to one of bemused judgment.

Chris still needed them to help look for Eddie. And he wanted her money. He couldn't confess what he thought he'd seen. He'd sound crazy, and she'd dismiss him.

"He must have run up the stairs faster than I realized."

Micah exchanged a glance with her heavyweight personal assistant. Roberts did a poorer job of hiding emotion. His eyes widened.

Chris wondered what had passed unspoken between them.

"You just missed him," Roberts grunted. "He came through before you and headed on outside."

"The basement must have spooked him," Micah added. "What did you find down there?"

"Now hold on," Dr. Terry removed his tweed jacket. "I didn't see Leon."

"You were still in the telephone room." Roberts gestured to the igloo with a huge thumb.

Dr. Terry furrowed his brow and tilted his head. "I suppose I was." He turned around to snap photos with his phone and write in a small leather notebook.

Chris caught his breath. The pond caught his attention. Its soft waves offered a welcome calm. "Leon passed through here?" It wasn't possible that he could have lost sight of Leon in the stairwell. But Micah's explanation was better than the alternative.

Micah helped pick up the blueprints. "Not sixty seconds before you showed up. He's just a little quicker than you."

"And he left?" Chris sat on the edge of a planter. He dropped his backpack onto the tile floor. Waving grass tickled the back of his neck.

Roberts squeezed the creases out of the rolled-up blueprints that Micah handed him. "Leon only planned on working a few hours. He's gotta get back to his main gig."

Micah's cheeks tightened. The movement barely visible, but Chris caught it.

Chris looked from her to the giant bodyguard. Roberts was avoiding Micah's glare. He'd picked up on her frustration with his claim about Leon.

It was a lie. An obvious one. Chris spoke before thinking, "Leon was having the time of his life down there. Never checked his watch once. I practically dragged him up."

Micah handed the last blueprint to Roberts. She folded her hands in front of her waist and locked eyes with Chris. "You found the blueprints you promised us. We should take a look. It might be enough to write you that check."

Chris understood how Micah Rayner could command a

boardroom. She wielded her angled features like a hatchet. Her voice evoked memories of every teacher, boss, and authority figure he'd ever feared. She exuded intelligent confidence. She didn't need to make threats because to oppose her will was to invite retribution on yourself.

But she was lying.

And she wasn't even trying to hide it.

The hubris of it stunned Chris.

He desperately wanted her to be telling the truth. Leon had sprinted ahead. But that's not what happened. Leon was there one moment, talking about his big plans to get back into building hacking, and then he was gone. And then the floor of the stairwell was gone, and something was lurching up the steps.

That had happened.

It meant this building contained something strange and dangerous. New technologies he couldn't understand.

It meant Eddie was in more danger beyond a breaking-and-entering charge.

Micah still stared at him, daring him to challenge her lie.

The question was how to best get her help to find Eddie. The $200k had taken a far back seat to that.

Chris broke eye contact. He looked at the pond, its gentle waves, and the illusion of an ocean horizon in the wall's reflection. He squeezed shut his eyes and looked away.

He didn't need calm. He needed focus.

The best way to get Micah to continue helping find Eddie was to continue helping her. Rich people like her saw every relationship as transactional. He could play that game.

"I'll show you what we found. Let's lay out the blueprints. And you'll want to see what I've got on this camera."

24

CHRIS WATCHED Micah watch the video.

The older woman sat on a planter, her wiry shoulders hunched over the digital camera. Roberts stood behind her to provide shade from the late morning sun that poured through the glass above the pond.

Dr. Terry still paced the courtyard, writing in his vain little notebook, as if the leather cover allowed the recording of more prestigious thoughts. He glanced their way every few minutes. His graying mustache twitched, and he did a poor job of hiding his jealousy that Micah was paying attention to Chris.

Chris stuck his tongue between his molars to avoid grinding his teeth. Eddie was probably on his way to the sixth floor. And when he didn't find any treasure, he'd head up to the thirty-first floor. That was, if Chris correctly remembered the video game.

He wanted to dash up after him, but this building was too big. Better if Micah's group was looking for him, too. And that meant giving Micah what she wanted. "Make sure you watch that thing moving in the last doorway."

"I see it," Micah said. "What do you think it is?"

"Hydraulic lift of some kind." Chris didn't believe that, but he thought it was closer to what Micah wanted to hear.

"Hmm." She tapped at the camera, replaying the video.

Chris didn't like the hesitation in her voice. She wasn't satisfied. "I have to go upstairs to look for my son. You'll keep an eye for him, too, right?"

Micah kept watching the video. She replied, distractedly, "Not yet. Let's see if there's schematics in those blueprints."

Chris gauged whether their help was worth delaying another minute. He decided it was. He started unrolling blueprints. Roberts crouched down to help.

The breeze in the courtyard ruffled the wide blue paper. They used supplies from Chris's bag to hold down the blueprints.

Within minutes, they'd laid the papers out between the planters. Over thirty sheets, held down against the wind by flashlights, spare batteries, a roll of duct tape, adjustable pliers, and everything else Chris had charged to Sherri's card this morning.

They were missing the two rolls of blueprints that Leon had taken with him outside.

That's not where he is.

Chris ignored the thought. He didn't know where Leon went, only that Micah was lying about him leaving. He couldn't do anything about that right now.

He jumped from blueprint to blueprint. Micah wanted more proof of the emptiness beneath sub-basement three. Maybe even designs for the lift system.

Roberts was staring down at a single blueprint. "You can read these?"

Chris thought he found what he was looking for but then realized it was the open space of the courtyard. "I've drawn similar ones myself. I'm an architect."

Dr. Terry scoffed. The old man still scribbled in his journal, but he'd moseyed closer to the blueprints to peek. Arrogant prick.

"Keep it to yourself." Chris turned his back on him. "Unless you've discovered something more helpful than video and blueprints. What are you even writing? Your grocery list? An acceptance speech for the awards you'll win after stealing work again?"

Behind Chris, Dr. Terry sniffed indignation. "You used to be a competent assistant. What happened?"

"I got screwed over." Chris spotted another blueprint. A cross-section like the one of the courtyard. Roberts must have laid it out—Chris didn't recognize it.

"You embarrassed yourself with your thesis." Dr. Terry was still talking. Chris didn't care. He'd found what he was looking for.

He snatched it up, held it against his chest, away from the wind, and took it to Micah.

Dr. Terry had pocketed his notebook. "Miss Rayner, isn't it time you cut this amateur loose?"

Roberts lumbered over next to Dr. Terry to rest an arm on the old man's tweed jacket. "Take it easy, huh?"

Chris spread out the blueprint in front of Micah. She lowered the camera, which she'd continued to watch on repeat. "I don't think you recorded any sort of lift. Whatever it is appears to be moving."

"That's probably just the light playing tricks." Chris hoped he wasn't wasting time, but he could take one more swing at recruiting her help. "Look at this."

The drawing showed a narrow rectangle in black, but instead of a bottom line, there were three small arrows indicating that the drawing continued on another page. In blue, two parallel lines bisected the rectangle. Chris pointed to them. "That's an elevator shaft."

"This is the whole building, then?" asked Micah.

"It's way weirder than that." Chris pointed to more blue lines at the top of the rectangle. "Those indicate HVAC ductwork. It's only above ground. And this is the empty space beneath the building."

Dr. Terry barged over. "You're reading that wrong." He leaned over, hands on knees, and chewed on his lip. "Well, I'll be. The drawing is simple enough for an amateur to read."

Micah looked at Dr. Terry. "You agree with Chris's assessment."

"A broken clock is right twice a day. The boy's right. There's no labels on the paper—which is unusual—but it fits what he says he saw downstairs, and what the video shows."

"That should be enough, right? There's evidence pointing to how they built this overnight. It wasn't overnight. They built it underground and then raised it up." Chris asked. He immediately knew he'd played his hand too soon.

Micah raised her eyebrows. "Eager, aren't we?"

"I told you, my son's in here somewhere. I'd like help to find him. But if you're still dragging your feet, I'm done. I'll go after him myself."

"Aren't you curious about who built this tower? And why?"

"Sure. On another day, when my wife hadn't just left me with our newly adopted son, and he hadn't just wandered off into whatever the hell this place is." He motioned to the courtyard around them.

The sun had stretched higher into the sky, shining down against the pond at a sharper angle. The bottoms of the skybridges above glowed with sunlight. The odd image relaxed him. He'd find Eddie. It'd all be fine.

"But I can't afford curiosity right now." He waved his phone between them. "I'm going to step outside to get service and make sure my son hasn't texted me. When I come back, I'm going upstairs. I've given you proof on how the building got here, so I'll expect that check, too."

Micah raised a hand to quiet him. The authority of such a small motion impressed him.

"I don't see any lifts," Micah said. "Nothing to raise it up. You haven't proven that the building was built underground and then raised up. Only that there's an open space below."

Chris squeezed his fists. "What else would that space be?"

Roberts patted Dr. Terry's shoulder. "There's an interesting question."

"You may have pointed us in the right direction," Micah said. "And if we find some sort of lifting mechanism, then that'll mean you've met the contract."

"Wonderful. Like I said, I'm going outside to check my phone."

"No. We go upstairs now." Micah's tone chilled him. Not a suggestion, not even an order, just a statement of how things were.

"If Eddie's left already, he'll have texted me."

Dr. Terry raised his index finger. "I'd like to see this open area beneath us. There'll be answers down there. For one, what's supporting this tower at all?"

Micah stood up. "We go upstairs."

"After I check my phone." Chris stepped towards the outer doors.

"If your son is still inside, then he's enjoying a rare privilege. We shouldn't interrupt." Micah motioned to Roberts.

The giant crossed the space between him and Chris in less than a second. Chris only had time to flinch before Roberts' bulk bore blocked out the bright courtyard. It was like a mountain about to tackle him.

Chris exhaled. Instead of leveling him, Roberts only grabbed his arm.

"Shit, I wasn't running." Chris tried to jerk away but it was like tugging against a freight train. "Why would I run? What the hell is going on?"

Micah was already walking to the elevator.

Dr. Terry's wide eyes looked from Chris to Micah. Frozen.

"We're going upstairs," Roberts said. He squeezed Chris's arm, lightly, but enough to show Chris had no choice. He whispered. "Your boy will be fine. This is a good place."

Chris had never heard something so wrong.

All morning, he'd had the nagging feeling that the tower was his. But that wasn't quite it.

Finally, the feeling solidified, and Chris realized he'd made a mistake. The tower didn't belong to him. He belonged to the tower.

"Gather up your equipment," Micah said, her back to them. "We'll need it."

25

—————

EDDIE AND CAM took the stairs.

In Treasure Hunter X, the elevators sometimes broke down, and then the security guards found you. The stairs were safer.

"My thighs are killing me." Cam leaned against the door to the sixth floor. "You sure we can't use the elevators?"

"Positive." He pointed to the big number six painted on the door. "The first hiding spot is in an office. In a safe behind a picture."

"Give me a second." Cam slid to the floor. "We should have brought some water bottles."

When they'd first entered the tower, they tried the basement first. But if Cam's buried money was down there, it was covered by a cement floor.

Plus it was dark, and they only had the flashlights on their cellphones.

"That was creepy as hell down there," Cam said as she caught her breath in the stairwell. "You really didn't hear anything?"

"No." Eddie had never been so freaked out by a basement before. But that's just because it was dark and huge. He hadn't heard anything.

"Are you lying right now?" Cam shook her head. "You can't tell me you didn't hear that. Someone was walking around down there, dragging their foot. We should have talked to them. They probably have my hundred-eighty dollars that I buried."

"You ran away."

Cam had gasped and then pushed Eddie back to the stairs, and practically dragged him up by his wrist. He'd been happy to follow.

Cam laughed. "Yeah, I freaked the fuck out. Probably a janitor or somebody. I guarantee you security is looking for us now."

"Security would have caught us by now. We're the only ones in here." He felt small in the tower's empty insides. If this was an office building, there should be people going to work. But maybe nobody expected it to get built so fast.

Eddie noticed Cam looking at him with a raised eyebrow. "But I'll be more helpful. I'll keep extra good lookout so security doesn't find us."

Cam rubbed his hair. "Hey, you either see them or you don't. Quit worrying so much about helping." Cam climbed back to her feet. "Let's go check this first hiding spot."

She opened the door onto the sixth floor.

Eddie's stomach filled with butterflies. The yucky kind.

It wasn't an office with desks and little short walls. It was the same open space as the first floor, but six floors up—a walkway around the edges, and a bridge across the middle. A warm air current blew up past his face.

This was all wrong.

He couldn't check the safe behind the picture in the third office from the door because there weren't any offices.

He should have known. It wouldn't be exactly the same as Treasure Hunter X. That was stupid. This was a real building.

"You forget to breathe?" Cam patted his cheek. "Your face is turning white."

"It's not what I thought." Eddie squeezed his eyes shut. This was turning into another cluster. Now Cam would leave and he'd have to search the building by himself.

"Breathe deep, little man. You got your facts mixed up, that's all. Could still be behind a picture. Look over there." She pointed across the bridge at a framed painting. She stepped onto the walkway and looked at the near wall. "Over here, too."

Eddie followed her onto the walkway. The air current blew stronger, like fingers through his hair. He avoided looking over the edge. He didn't like heights.

Cam was already pulling down the first picture. It was a black and white photograph of the new building from outside. "How fast did they snap this photo? This place is weird as shit."

The wall behind the picture was blank.

"Let's try the others," said Cam. "And if there's nothing there, maybe you heard wrong. Could be the sixteenth floor, God help my legs. Plus, there's other hiding spots you know about, right?"

Eddie nodded. He hadn't heard wrong because it wasn't the man in the driveway who'd shared the hiding spots. He knew the hiding spots from Treasure Hunter X. But same difference. He went to the next picture and peeked behind it. Nothing.

"See? It's all good. You're helpful." Cam quickly grabbed his chin and made him look her in the eye. "But you don't have to be."

He did, though. So he would be.

They continued their search.

26

———

THE ELEVATOR RIDE shouldn't have lasted this long. It made no sense.

Chris stood in front of the closed doors. His refilled backpack weighed heavy on his shoulders. He cradled his prybar and a roll of blueprints in his arms.

Roberts breathed down on the top of Chris's head, close enough to grab him in case he decided to run once the doors opened.

Micah stood at Roberts' other side, and Dr. Terry made himself small in the back corner of the elevator.

Chris wanted to get out of this elevator, find Eddie, and get out of this building.

But first, he wanted to know what the hell Micah and Roberts were up to.

"Where are we going?" he demanded.

"Up," Roberts said.

"What's upstairs?"

"Hopefully, evidence revealing the purpose of this tower," Micah said.

"It's an office building," Chris said. "Commercial space. Cubicles, water coolers, and slowly drained hopes and dreams."

Roberts said, "Can't be. Those sorts of buildings already exist. This is something new."

"Why do you think that?" Chris asked. "Because of how it was constructed?"

Micah cut off that thread of conversation. "I'm altering the terms of the contract. How it was constructed no longer matters. Now I want to know why. What's this building *do*?"

"First of all, I met your contract already. Secondly, I'm here to find my son and get him back outside."

Roberts leaned against Chris. The man must have weighed half a ton. "This is today's job. Better if you accept it. This is a good place. Your son is safe."

Chris's back went stiff. Roberts was speaking nonsense. Couldn't he feel how *wrong* this building was? He watched Micah's cold eyes, searching for her intentions. "You're holding back. You know things about this building."

"But not yet enough," Micah said.

The elevator slowed, a bell dinged, and the doors slid open.

27

———

CHRIS WOULD HAVE SPRINTED for the stairs, but Roberts had a firm grip on his shoulder. Chris had to get away from him.

But the room was moving.

The lobby immediately outside the elevator was still. Dull tile floors and a drop-ceiling, like the lobby on the ground floor.

A narrow hallway hugged the building's outside wall, probably connecting to the next elevator lobby.

But in front of them, through glass doors, was the central floor.

In a way, Chris had been right: this was commercial office space. Through the glass, there was an open floor of writing desks. It reminded Chris of reporters' bullpens in old movies. To one side, a maze of cubicles. To the other, a wall of private offices, solid wood doors and frosted windows.

Everything moved.

Dr. Terry cursed and exhaled a raspy moan. Chris thought he should share his terror, but he couldn't wrap his mind around what he was seeing.

The desk closest to him was blue painted steel. Large enough to hold a lamp and typewriter. Its surface swirled like oil atop still water. Chris watched one swirl reach the edge of the desktop, then instead of disappearing like it would do if it were an effect of the light, it turned ninety degrees to continue down the desk's leg. When it reached the carpeted floor, it shifted color to match the gray carpet fibers, and it joined the ocean of swirling movement on the floor.

That swirl was one of thousands on the desk, all sliding and stretching against each other, covering the desk in its entirety. The desk was one of a hundred in the disorienting bullpen.

Chris walked forward but stopped short of opening a glass door.

Roberts let him go. "I never woulda thought..."

It wasn't just the desk. Every surface in the open room was swirling movement.

The whole thing felt welcoming, like an active forest inviting hikers to focus on a million tiny movements and forget their outside problems. In fact, tall wooden filing cabinets against the walls, green vine patterns in the wallpaper, and low-hanging, vine-like light fixtures all furthered the illusion of a forest.

Last spring, Chris and Eddie had driven out to the Shenandoah Mountains. Sherri had stayed home, putting in extra work on the weekend. They'd picked a trail, not expecting the "difficult" rating to live up to its name. But while Chris's thighs ached, and while he worried about Eddie's sharp breaths which puffed out the boy's rosy cheeks, he'd been happy. The canopy of pines and oaks, the thick undergrowth, the enveloping jagged hills and gullies—it all felt like a protective blanket. He could pull the woods over his head and protect himself from the monsters back home: poverty and failure.

The thirty-first floor of the new skyscraper recreated that feeling.

Chris took another step towards the glass doors separating him from the bullpen.

The artificial forest tried to calm him, but it wasn't enough.

Hiking Shenandoah with his son had been a healthy respite from stress at home, on a weekend, after a busy week spent applying for jobs. If he let this office relax him, he'd be fleeing a problem that needed immediate attention.

Two problems, actually: getting away from Roberts and then finding Eddie.

Roberts touched the handle of the glass door. He watched the room intently.

Chris looked over his shoulder. Three elevator doors behind him, one open. No doors to stairwells. He looked down the narrow hallways on either side of the lobby. No sign of stairs, but they had to be somewhere.

Micah, who stood next to a hunched-over Dr. Terry by the open elevator door, noticed Chris looking around. She stepped in front of the elevator. "Roberts?"

The big man grunted.

"Step aside so Chris and Dr. Terry can investigate the room."

A plan sprung to life. Chris did not want to go inside the shifting room. But he could see straight across it. There was another set of glass doors on the opposite side. Another lobby. An escape route.

But he couldn't act excited and give away his plan. "Why us? Why aren't you going?"

"Because we've hired Dr. Terry for his architectural expertise."

Roberts finally looked away from the glass. "And you're still after that open contract."

"I've completed it." Chris readied the misdirect. "I've given you evidence about how it was built. If you want me to keep investigating for information about *why*, then we need another contract."

"I can offer a bonus atop the current contract. How's another fifty-thousand sound?"

Chris didn't expect her to agree that easily. But the important part was that she believed he was satisfied with the money. "Record yourself agreeing to that. Then text it to me. And make it a hundred thousand."

Roberts said, "You can't negotiate. What's your leverage?"

Chris didn't say, "leaving," because then Roberts would try to stop him.

"It's fine," Micah said. She held her phone up like she was taking a selfie. "I agree to add a bonus payment of a hundred thousand dollars, on the condition that Chris Haberman finds the purpose of this building."

"Or finds evidence that leads to finding the purpose," Chris added.

Micah repeated that then ended the video. She sent the recording to Chris via bluetooth. He made a scene verifying that the recording came through.

Chris tucked the blueprints between his back and his backpack. "We'll let you know what we find. Dr. Terry, you coming?"

The old professor tugged at his mustache. "I'm afraid I have other responsibilities at the university to tend to today."

Roberts sighed. He picked up Dr. Terry around the shoulders and carried him to the glass.

Chris opened the door, then Roberts set the petrified Dr. Terry inside. Chris entered behind him.

The door slammed shut.

28

INSIDE THE SWIRLING ROOM, the relaxing effect was instant.

The urgency Chris felt dripped away. He made himself hang onto his stress over Eddie. While this building tried to relax him, it also had his son.

Dr. Terry even leaned on the closest desk to catch his breath. "That ogre," he muttered before slowly exhaling.

Chris looked at his feet. The shifting surface patterns on the carpet made his shoes look like still boats in rough water.

The more he thought about it, taking time to relax wouldn't be running from his problems. Eddie would be fine. A little relaxation would be good for the boy.

And Chris's other issues were mostly his own damaged ego from years of failure. Job interviewers picked up on that. Eddie would pick up on it. Chris's fear of not giving Eddie a stable home would make their home feel less stable. So calming his mind was in itself a solution.

Chris purposely ground his teeth. He wasn't ready to calm down yet. The room no longer felt artificial; it felt as natural as his hike through Shenandoah. But he needed to get away from Micah and Roberts, find Eddie, and get home. And all that meant staying alert and on edge. "Here's what we're going to do."

Dr. Terry looked up. The swirling surfaces around him made his profile a still silhouette. He sniffed indignantly, then he relaxed. "Yes, you've always been keen on mundane logistics. Let's hear it."

"Cut the attitude. I could leave you here."

The professor's wide eyes peered back into the lobby. Under the hum of fluorescent lights, Micah and Roberts watched them. "They won't let us leave. We should call the police." He squeezed his eyes shut and shook his head. "But this has to be some kind of misunderstanding. That's Micah Rayner! She's been on the cover of Time Magazine."

"So I'll leave you here, then?"

"No," Dr. Terry said quickly. "What's your plan?"

"They need to see us investigating. So we investigate." Chris opened the drawers of the first desk. Empty.

Dr. Terry walked into the nearest cubicle. "This is your plan? Do what they want?"

"Work your way across the room. To the doors on the far side."

Chris looked up at the low chandeliers. The chains they hung from had thin metal leaves. He wasn't even sure what "purpose" an office building could have. Contain offices. Be a comfortable space. Relax its occupants.

Maybe there'd be something in the offices, behind the solid wood doors and frosted glass.

A shadow moved behind the glass.

Chris's mind went to Leon, already up here trying to find

answers before Chris could. Micah's ace in the hole to avoid paying Chris. He walked over to open the office door.

Chris's steps felt lighter. If Leon was okay, then maybe the building wasn't dangerous. Eddie was still safe.

The figure behind the glass moved again. Lurched.

Chris stopped breathing. The swirling surfaces surrounded him, smothering.

Something was in that office. The same thing in sub-basement three and in the stairwell right after Leon disappeared.

He backed away.

The shadow on the glass moved. Up, over, down. Towards the door.

Chris got behind a desk.

The office door creaked open. Soft light inside.

The room swirled in time with Chris's pounding heart.

A moment passed. Another.

The open door was a threat. Any moment, the foreign thing would lurch into view.

It didn't.

Chris crept back to the next desk. "Dr. Terry," he hissed.

After there was no response, Chris chanced a quick glance over his shoulder, then back to the open office door.

In the nearest cubicle, Dr. Terry sat in a chair, eyes closed, hands folded over his stomach.

Chris hurried across the room to him. He smacked his shoulder. "Wake up."

"I'm awake. Simply enjoying this chair. If I had one in my office, my students would wait months for their grades."

The professor was falling more smoothly into the room's calming effect.

"There's something in here with us." From this angle,

Chris saw deeper into the open office. A desk, floor lamp, landscape photo on the wall. Everything but one corner. Enough space for the lurching thing to be waiting. "I think it's dangerous. We should keep moving."

But Dr. Terry only sighed. "I owe you an apology. Several apologies, I think."

"Now's not the time."

Roberts tapped on the glass. He motioned to the open door, then shrugged his shoulders to ask, *what's in there?*

Dr. Terry cleared his throat. "I have a tendency to think only of my reputation. I hope you understand. When you're a professor, your reputation is your career. But I should have balanced that against treating others right. In your case, I failed at that, and I apologize. Really, what matters is being at peace with yourself. And for some reason, I'm feeling that now."

Chris yanked him by the armpits to his feet.

He groggily opened his eyes. A smile cupped his mustache. "You're right. We should leave. We'll come back later when that brute out there has calmed down."

"Sure," Chris said. He guided Dr. Terry through the maze of desks, keeping an eye on the office door.

Behind him, Roberts pounded on the glass. It didn't matter if Micah and Roberts realized what they were doing. They had the head start to make it to the next elevator bank.

"Would you like to hear the irony of my behavior towards you?" He took Chris's silence as an affirmative. "I was so afraid that your odd thesis would tarnish my reputation. After all, the idea of the Flat Iron Building being an imitation is absurd. Let alone an imitation of a structure in rural Vietnam. They didn't even have the infrastructure to deliver the materials."

Chris had heard these insults a hundred times. He'd been duped by a bizarre conspiracy theory. He'd moved past it. Although his career hadn't.

They reached the glass doors on the opposite end of the room.

"But here's the ironic part. Micah Rayner believes the same thing. And not just about the Flatiron Building! The Crystal Palace, the Tremont Hotel, and long before our modern cities. The Tower of London, copied from an alleged stone fortress in northern Scotland. Pliny the Elder's first Roman greenhouses, stolen from already existing structures in Carthage. Even ancient smokehouses—historians can't decide what century they first appeared, but Micah claims she has evidence that the very first one did, in fact, *appear*."

Chris stopped at the door, still keeping an eye on the office. Micah had apparently shared much more with Dr. Terry. "What are you saying?"

"According to Micah, this isn't the first building to appear overnight."

29

CHRIS TRIED to digest Dr. Terry's confession.

This wasn't the first building to appear overnight. Micah hadn't just caught word of this tower and quickly decided to reverse engineer its construction. She was expecting this. Ready for it.

To what end?

Discovering its "purpose?"

The idea made Chris uneasy, even in this calming, swirling office. For a wildly successful billionaire, Micah had behaved erratically.

She lied about the contract of reverse-engineering the construction and hid her true goal of finding the building's purpose.

And she'd essentially kidnapped Chris and Dr. Terry to do so. A woman who ran multiple giant corporations couldn't behave impulsively like that. Which meant this tower had brought out another side of her. She was unpredictable. Dangerous. And she had that leashed ogre to enforce her whims.

Now, Dr. Terry was saying that Micah believed in those same conspiracies that derailed Chris's career.

That changed nothing. She was dangerous, and Eddie was still in here somewhere.

"Forget it," he said.

Dr. Terry hugged him. "Thank you for accepting my apology. I promise I've got some soul-searching to do."

"No, I meant forget all that about Micah believing my thesis. Let's get out and then we'll talk about it." Chris opened the glass door. He pulled Dr. Terry out of the disorienting bullpen of shifting surfaces and into a plain elevator lobby.

Except there were no elevators.

The dull cinderblock walls had metal frames where an elevator door would open, but they were solid cinderblock inside. No buttons on the wall.

Chris turned around. Across the bullpen, through the glass doors opposite this one, Micah screamed at them. He couldn't hear her, but the fury in her wide eyes was evident. She yelled at Roberts, stopped him from cutting through the central room, then waved him down the side hallway.

She yelled something else at Chris, then took the other hallway.

They were circling the building to reach them.

"But you do forgive me, right?" Dr. Terry rubbed his shoulders. "Or you'll try to? Obviously, it'll take time. The important thing is, it's not about my reputation. It's about being at peace with myself. And I'd be more at peace if you forgave me."

"They're coming after us." If Chris was going to risk running into one of them, better it be the frail sixty-year-old.

He tugged Dr. Terry down the hallway. "We need to find the stairs before they find us."

Dr. Terry hurried after him. "Here's an idea. I'll work my Rolodex to find you more work. I hurt your career, so I'll do my best to repair it."

"Sure, that'll be great." The hallway was low, narrow, and dark. The air was still, with a smell of mildew. Thirty yards ahead, it ended in another lobby.

They reached the lobby. The hallway turned to run down the next side of the building. In the lobby, yellow lights revealed a single elevator door. Chris mashed the down button.

"Micah!" Dr. Terry's cheery voice sent a chill down Chris's back.

He turned to see Micah striding towards them, reddish-gray hair flowing behind. She held something small and black—a taser, or maybe pepper spray. Chris couldn't tell with her still in the dark hallway.

Chris pressed the down button repeatedly.

Back the way they'd came, way down past the first lobby, Roberts' bulky form lumbered toward them.

Trapped.

The elevator groaned somewhere above. Pulleys squeaked.

Dr. Terry walked to meet Micah. "Let's take a breath for a moment. We all want the same thing." He paused for a second like a thought had just occurred to him. "I can do so much for your organization. I'm destined for great things."

A shimmering violet mass bulged out of the wall. Organic, pulsing. It enveloped Dr. Terry, flattened against the tile floor, lost substance.

Chris stared, slack-jawed, at Micah Rayner. Her eyes widened. She covered her mouth with wrinkled hands.

The hallway between them was empty. The wall and floor were clean, with no sign of any organic, shimmering mass. Dr. Terry was gone.

30

—————

ROBERTS CRASHED into Chris from behind.

The tile floor rushed up to meet him. Pain exploded in his shoulder.

Animal instinct took over. Chris fought to escape not Roberts but the cold tile.

"Let me up," he pleaded. His cheek rubbed on the floor, over a bump. Chris gasped, expecting the bump to grow and rise.

The giant bodyguard pinned Chris tighter.

The bump remained a bump.

Micah issued a breathless order. "We keep moving."

Roberts hauled Chris to his feet. "Where to?" he asked.

Chris pulled his backpack taught against his back and rearranged the blueprints that Roberts had creased. He held his prybar tight. He considered swinging it into Roberts' knee, but he feared the big man would absorb the blow and retaliate.

He couldn't run. Roberts was too close. And even if he

did, what was stopping that thing from taking him, like it had Dr. Terry?

And Leon.

"Is that what happened to Leon?" he asked.

Chris's lungs pumped faster as he realized, "My son is in here. Forget your exploration. I have to get Eddie out."

Roberts shoved Chris to follow Micah. He had no choice until they gave him an opening. He squeezed his fists around the crowbar.

"Did you know it would happen?" Chris demanded.

Roberts answered him from behind. "We didn't know." His deep voice sounded genuinely remorseful.

"Even after Leon?"

Micah raised a hand. "Stop talking," she whispered.

"The situation has become dangerous," Roberts said. "I make the calls until we're in the clear. If Chris is going to help us find answers, he needs information. The more we tell him, the quicker this goes."

Micah ignored him. They reached the corner of the building. Another lobby devoid of elevators or stairs. They turned, headed towards the elevator bank where they'd first come up.

"Boss," Roberts repeated. "Chris needs information."

"Keep your information to yourself because I'm not helping you." He imagined swinging the crowbar at Roberts' knees. "My son's in here. As soon as we find some stairs, I'm going to find him."

Micah walked faster. Chris tried to keep himself in the center of the hallway, as far as possible from either wall.

"Boss," Roberts said, "are we on the same page?"

Micah whirled around. "Chris is hired labor. A tool. Don't put him on the same level as us."

Chris made himself small. Farther from the walls, and it let his captors focus on each other.

Roberts had set aside his submissiveness. "I don't care what you call him. I want to know what this new building can do. But it's obviously dangerous. To keep you safe, I'm finishing this job as soon as possible. If more information helps Chris find us answers more quickly, then we give him more information."

Micah tapped her taser against her open palm. "The more he knows, the more likely he'll get in the way."

"In the way of what?" Roberts asked. "We don't even know what this is yet."

"I'm starting to get an idea," Micah said. "Let's not discuss this here. The elevator may be safer."

"How about outside?" Chris said. "Outside would be safest."

"Whatever took Dr. Terry and Leon," Roberts said, "that was in the outer hallways. We should go in there." He tapped the wall between them and the bullpen.

"No," Chris said, "there's something in there." Whatever he'd seen lurching behind the frosted glass and in the sub-basement was different from what had taken Dr. Terry. More defined. More intentioned in its movement.

"I agree with the architect," Micah said. "I suspect the tower's central spaces may be more dangerous than the outer corridors, even with the hazards that have taken our friends."

Roberts nodded, and they headed for the elevator.

31

———

As THEY REACHED the lobby and moved into the elevator, Chris looked again into the bullpen.

The glass walls separating it from the lobby now swirled with the same surface movement as everything inside.

Chris backed away toward the elevator. "Is it spreading?"

"Or it's reaching for us." Roberts pulled Chris into the elevator.

Micah stood in the lobby, head cocked to the side, watching the shifting glass.

"You just said it was dangerous, boss. Let's go."

She turned and briskly walked to join them.

The doors slid shut.

Chris reached for the ground floor button, but Roberts' meaty hand gripped his wrist. "Where to, boss?"

"Up. One floor at a time."

Roberts cleared his throat. "How about we put a few floors between us and that LSD kaleidoscope stuff, in case it's pursuing us?"

Micah nodded.

Chris lunged again for the ground floor button. Roberts shoved him backwards.

The elevator walls felt tighter than before. The sensation of movement tugged at Chris as the elevator carried him farther from the exit, father from home, farther from Eddie. Panic creeped in at the edges. "You gotta let me leave. I can't help you here. I design minor renovations or backyard cottages. I don't know anything about this."

"You know more than you think," Micah said.

"My thesis? I summarized some crazy articles I read online. I'm no expert. Listen, I've got a son to find. Don't you have kids?"

"Yes, you told us about Eddie," Micah said. "If all goes well, we'll help collect him and escort you outside."

"Are you lying to me?" Chris turned to Roberts. "Is she lying?"

Veins in Roberts' neck tensed. "We don't know what we're looking for or how long it'll take to find. Maybe we shouldn't let a kid wander around in here. We can't guarantee how long we'll be."

His honesty flipped a switch inside Chris. "Can't guarantee how long? You can't even guarantee our safety! Look at Dr. Terry! Or Leon!"

"It will be worth it," Micah said.

"Worth their lives?"

"If they're dead, then yes." Micah spat the words, responding to Chris's anger in kind.

Roberts turned to Micah. "That was an accident, not a sacrifice."

Chris couldn't resist the opportunity of the back of Roberts' head exposed, defenseless. He didn't have space to rear back the prybar, so he jabbed it, wedge-first, at Roberts' skull, throwing all his weight into it.

The iron impacted above the giant's ear. It broke skin to scrape against the bone. Bright blood poured down his ear onto his shirt.

He staggered into the wall but caught himself.

Chris jumped forward, taking advantage of the space he'd just claimed to rear back this time.

His whole body went tense. Electricity hijacked his muscles. He collapsed. The prybar clanged to the tile floor.

Micah stood over him with her taser. "How bad is it?" she asked.

Roberts groaned. "Give me a minute."

Chris tried to move but only twitched. He'd blown his chance. No way Roberts would turn his back again.

By the time Chris could sit up, Roberts was standing over him with a rag pressed to the side of his head. Fury in his eyes, then self-control.

"Listen, Micah," he said. "This is what he's going to do. It's what I would do if I didn't know what I know. Let's bring him in and maybe he'll get on board."

Micah pressed an elevator button and the car jerked to a stop. "Fine. Show him what we have so far."

32

Eddie's legs were jelly.

He was thirsty.

And he was getting nervous.

They trudged up the stairs, finally reaching the sixteenth floor.

Cam still led the way. She carried her coat. Sweat darkened the back of her red shirt. She pressed her hand against the white cinderblock wall for support.

The stairwell had cement steps. Bare lightbulbs at every landing lit the stairs in a queasy yellow.

"For how fancy it is with all the rooms and offices," Cam said, breathing heavy, "these stairs are worse than a cheap parking garage."

They'd searched several floors below. Regular offices, like on TV, but nothing behind any pictures.

Eddie had felt less helpful with every patch of bare wall they uncovered.

They'd tried some of the other hiding spots from stage 3

of Treasure Hunter X: in a desk drawer, under a potted plant, in a toilet tank, and on top of a bookshelf.

Nothing.

Cam still sounded cheery and hopeful, but Eddie knew she was forcing it. The butterflies in Eddie's gut fluttered faster. Cam's patience would run out. Then he'd be up here all alone.

The building was empty and dull. Eddie hated it. Something about the way the offices were set up. So perfectly uniform. Desks every three feet. Water coolers every fifty feet. Like the whole building was printed out.

But he'd only seen offices on TV, so maybe this was just how they were normally.

Cam grabbed the door handle for the sixteenth floor and waited. "This one feels lucky, right?"

Eddie nodded since that's what she wanted.

She opened the door.

She inhaled sharply and stepped back.

Eddie looked inside.

Another office. Short cubicle walls lined in beige carpet. Potted plants marked the regular intersections of the walkways. Tall black bookshelves along the outer walls. No windows.

A stranger stood in the middle of the walkway.

He stood atop a chair and was sliding a tile back into the ceiling.

His khaki pants had pockets all over. He wore a backpack, which adults didn't usually do.

Security.

Eddie's legs tensed. They were caught. They'd never run fast enough.

But security guards wore uniforms. And Eddie didn't think they'd look as angry as this man did. His lips curled up in a sneer.

And there was something wrong with his eyes. His head pointed at Cam and then Eddie, but his eyes moved around too much.

"You kids shouldn't be up here. Did Micah send you?"

Eddie recognized that name. The man in the driveway had mentioned her. Dad knew who she was.

Cam stood straight so she looked taller. "Yeah, he sent us."

The man sneered. "Micah's a woman."

Cam shrugged. "I just got the email. Haven't met her in person."

The butterflies in Eddie's gut fluttered up into his throat. Cam was a terrible liar.

The man grunted. He licked his sneering lips.

He didn't believe her. Eddie got ready to run. In Treasure Hunter X, when the guards spotted him, he almost never got away. Dad was good at escaping, but Eddie always got too nervous and his sweaty thumbs slipped off the controller.

When the guards caught you, they'd throw you outside. But this man wasn't a security guard. He was just angry. Angry adults were dangerous.

The man walked towards them. "You have any luck yet?"

Cam snuck a hand onto Eddie's back. Her fingers dug into his shoulder. They nudged him towards the stairs, then gripped him firmly. *Be ready to run, but not yet.*

Eddie wanted to spew. He never escaped the guards. But he couldn't tell that to Cam without this guy hearing.

"No luck yet," Cam said. "What about you?"

The man kept walking towards them. His eyes jumped

around like he was spotting a million fireflies. "Tell me what you've seen so far."

Eddie pulled towards the stairs. Cam held him back.

They needed to start running now. Without a head start, the man would easily catch them.

"We've looked in all the hiding spots below us," Cam said.

"Hiding spots?" His thick eyebrows furrowed over his dancing eyes.

As he got closer, he broke into a sprint. Cam tried to jerk away, but the man grabbed her arm.

"Ow!" she cried. "Get the fuck off me."

He dragged her through the doorway.

Eddie froze. Cam had let go of him. The stairs were open. He could run.

"What'd you find?" The man shook Cam by her shoulders. "How's it work?"

"How's what work?"

He threw her to the floor. He put his boot on her stomach. "If you got the email from Micah, then you know. I can't find shit in here, but I'm not walking out empty-handed."

Eddie wanted to run. But Cam was nice. He had to do something.

He knew the only way to calm down an angry adult:

Be helpful.

He stepped through the doorway into the office. "I can help you."

The man looked Eddie up and down. At least, his head made the movement. His eyes couldn't stay still. "This place isn't for you."

That was the same weird thought he'd had earlier. Chills chased away the butterflies. The building didn't feel so empty anymore. Something here didn't want him here. No, that wasn't quite it. The building didn't care about him.

That didn't make any sense.

While the man waited for Eddie to respond, Cam quietly scooted away.

"I can help you," Eddie repeated. "But you can't hurt Cam."

"How can you help if this place isn't for you?"

Cam crawled to her feet. "The fuck are you talking about?"

The man whipped his head around. "How'd you get so far away? Come back over here and tell me what you've found. I can't make heads or tails of it."

Cam was only a few feet away. Eddie realized the man might be on drugs. When his old mom's friends were on drugs, that was when it was most important to be helpful.

"I'll tell you all the hiding places," Eddie said. "But then you have to leave us alone."

"What's in these hiding places? Blueprints? That'd be enough for Micah, I bet. But I want to see footage of the construction."

Cam carefully walked over to Eddie's side. He liked her hand on his shoulder. This guy was bad news, but Cam was practically an adult, and she saw how helpful Eddie was, which meant she'd protect him. "I don't think he's looking for treasure," she whispered.

"Treasure?" The man scratched his cheek.

Eddie nodded. "I know all the hiding spots. It's not in the same place every time."

The man raised one finger. "You get it! This place is too many places at once. Not the same place."

Eddie wrung his hands. He was trying to be helpful, but

something was wrong with this man. Maybe more than drugs.

"So tell me the hiding spots with the secrets."

"On floor six, behind a painting in the third office from the door. On floor nine, in a safe in the floor under the rug, right in the middle of everything." Eddie kept listing off the hiding places, even the ones they'd already checked, even though he knew this building wasn't exactly like Treasure Hunter X.

"You're very helpful." The man's eyes finally stopped their frantic movement. They focused on Eddie. His gaze was like being smothered by a blanket. "You'll come with me."

He reached for Eddie, gnawed fingernails filling Eddie's vision as the man somehow reached from ten feet away, fingertips about to brush Eddie's nose.

"You can fuck off." Cam yanked Eddie behind her, putting herself between him and the man. Eddie fell onto his butt. Cam threw a chair at the man, then dragged Eddie by his shirt back through the door. His collar scratched his neck.

The man rolled on the floor, holding his knee and cursing. He went still. He locked eyes on Eddie again. "Are you helpful?" he growled.

Cam slammed shut the door.

She pulled Eddie to his feet, then towards the stairs going down.

That was the way out. Eddie wanted to run away. Downstairs, out the door, and back home. Back to Chris. Dad.

But if he didn't find the treasure, there wouldn't be a home. "No. We haven't found the treasure yet."

"That guy's dangerous." Cam pointed to the closed door. "Did you see his eyes? And how'd he reach you like that?"

Eddie didn't want to think about that. It wasn't even that something weird had happened when the man grabbed at him. It was that Eddie was being helpful—the man *said* he was helpful—and it still wasn't good enough. If being helpful wasn't enough for one adult, would it be good enough for Chris?

It had to be. He wanted to stay with Chris.

He pulled Cam toward the stairs leading up. "I have to find the treasure for my dad. You hurt that guy's leg. He can't follow us upstairs."

Cam sang a nonsense tune to herself, deciding. "You're crazy. But I need that money, too. Okay, let's go. But we find different stairs on the way back down."

They headed farther up.

EDDIE TRIED to see on Cam's face if she was mad at him. "I tried to be helpful. He was still mean."

"I told you about that already," Cam said. "There's you, and there's what you can do for other people. And those aren't the same thing."

"I'm sorry." He didn't say it, but she was wrong again. You did have to be helpful. He was sure of it. But now he'd done his best, and it didn't matter.

"Quit thinking about that. Let's find your treasure."

Even though they were going up, Eddie had the distinct thought that they were getting deeper.

Their footsteps echoed in the cement stairwell. Eddie's head was starting to hurt from being thirsty. His legs felt tight.

He could be strong. Once they found the treasure, everything would be okay.

And maybe Cam was a little bit right. Maybe sometimes, or for some adults, he just could never be helpful enough. And maybe that meant being helpful wasn't the most important thing.

That same weird thought came into his head. *This place isn't for you.* This time, it was followed by: *But it could be.*

The building didn't feel empty. Not full, either. It just was. Exactly what it was meant to be.

33

CHRIS SAT in the corner of the elevator. He had nowhere to run, and if he was honest with himself, he was curious. He couldn't explain the swirling surfaces of the office bullpen. He couldn't explain how a sixty-story building could be supported by an empty pit. Or what he'd seen lurching in the basement and office.

Or how a skyscraper had appeared in a residential neighborhood overnight.

He could do nothing in this moment to get out and find Eddie.

So with his main goal temporarily thwarted, he leaned into curiosity. Maybe something they told him would help him escape.

Micah stood in the opposite corner of the stopped elevator, arms crossed.

Roberts tied off the rag around his head. He winced. He pulled an iPad from his shoulder bag, unlocked it, and handed it to Chris. "Let's talk about your thesis."

"Dr. Terry said you agreed with it. That the Flatiron building wasn't the first steel-framed skyscraper."

"The architect, Daniel Burnham, had recently returned from a trip to Vietnam, or French Indochina, which it was called at the time. A rural highland area called Da Lat. In 1895, its population was less than a thousand. One hundred seventy miles of dirt mountain roads to get there. But somehow, there was a steel skyscraper on the edge of town. The locals couldn't explain how it got there." He pointed to the iPad. "Look in 'Files,' then 'Flatiron.'"

Chris navigated to an image. It was a scan of a faded charcoal sketch on yellowed paper. The sketch showed a triangular building, at least fifteen stories. Around it were homes on log stilts, braided branches for walls, and roofs of thick bundled grasses. Someone had drawn the Flatiron building in an old Vietnamese village.

"This would have helped in my thesis. Who drew it?"

"My great-grandfather," Micah said. "He'd been searching, the same way I've been searching. But where he was hoping for another step on the journey, I knew I'd find the journey's culmination."

"Granddaddy Rayner showed his sketch to Daniel Burnham," said Roberts, "and Burnham happily took credit for designing the first steel-framed skyscraper. It changed everything. Cities could now expand upwards instead of just sprawling outward. That development did more to tightly pack people together than anything else in history."

"How do you know this is real?" Chris asked. "You've got more detail than I ever found, but I thought all this was proven to be a hoax. Anyone could have sketched this."

"I still have the original," Micah said. "We've dated the paper. It matches my family's claims."

"And we're just getting started here," Roberts said. "Look for a folder labeled 'Advancements.'"

Chris found it. More images.

"Two more requirements before cities could become as dense as they are today."

"Air conditioning and plumbing," Chris said. "You're telling me the Larkin Administration Building was a ripoff? Frank Lloyd Wright was a fraud?"

"His aesthetic designs are his own," Micah said. "But the concept of designing a building around air conditioning—which skyscrapers need for their top levels to avoid getting superheated by the sun—that was stolen from a building that appeared overnight in rural Idaho."

"Air conditioning already existed. It was only a matter of time before someone stuck it in a large building."

"True," Micah said, "but the Idaho building made it happen quicker. It helped man's natural development hurry past the trial-and-error phase."

Chris opened an image labeled, "Tremont."

He recognized the sketch. Tremont House, a four-story hotel in Boston. It was a neo-classical manor, with columns supporting the porch roof. The first hotel—and building of its size—to feature indoor plumbing. But the sketch wasn't in Boston. The hotel was surrounded by sand dunes instead of Boston streets.

"And where was this one?" Chris asked, more skeptical by the moment.

"The Sonoran Desert," Micah said. "This one is an artist's

recreation after interviewing men who claimed to have seen it."

"Let me guess," Chris said. "Somehow, one of those men was connected to the Tremont House architect." Dr. Terry would have known his name, but Chris didn't.

"Bingo," Roberts said. "One played cards with Isaiah Rogers."

That name sounded familiar.

"Again," Micah said, "this advancement would have happened eventually. But this overnight appearance quickened it."

"What are you saying?" Chris asked. "Skyscrapers were a gift from God?"

"Perhaps something akin to that," Micah said.

"Skyscrapers are only the newest examples of this phenomenon," Roberts said.

Chris said, "Dr. Terry mentioned the Tower of London and ancient Roman greenhouses."

"Correct," Micah said. "Historians credit the Romans with creating the first greenhouses. A major step in allowing the centralization of food cultivation. Not to mention the large plate glass that was also essential for modern urban buildings. But my family has uncovered writings that mention greenhouses in Carthage ten years before Rome's. And while western records show the Tower of London as being the first medieval castle, my private library holds records describing a similar structure in northern Scotland, ten years before construction began in London."

"Sometimes historians mess up," Chris said.

"Patterns denote intention," Micah said. "Mesopotamian smokehouses appeared too suddenly in history. If it had been a natural development, meat would have first been smoked in caves, or pits."

"Can you prove it wasn't?"

Micah ignored him. "Even simple Native American palisade designs, I have evidence that they *found* this style of construction and then replicated it."

Roberts motioned to the iPad, where Chris found notes on Cahokian walled cities.

Chris asked the obvious problem that'd been bothering him. "So where are they now? Where's this Scottish Tower of London? That's made of stone. It should still be there. And where's the evidence of Carthage greenhouses? Or what about the hotel in the Sonoran desert? That was only two hundred years ago. Can we go see it? And what about Frank Lloyd Wright's supposed inspiration in Idaho? Or the Flatiron original in Vietnam? If what you're saying is true, where's the buildings? That's why my thesis destroyed my career—there's nothing there!"

"They don't last," Micah said. "The tower in Scotland appeared to be stone to everyone who explored it. And for the builders who inspected the design, it was everything they needed to learn how to do it themselves. But it crumbled within months."

"That's insane," Chris said.

"Crazier than that Picasso room?" Roberts pointed at the elevator wall.

"Yes!"

Micah wasn't deterred from her alternate history lesson. "The same with the air-conditioned building in rural Idaho. It stood long enough for men to make notes of the airflow system. Then it fell to pieces, which dissolved in the rain. The same in Vietnam. And in the Sonoran Desert, except there it was swallowed by the sand."

"There'd still be records," Chris said.

"There are. You have scans of them in front of you."

"These are amateur sketches and notes from lunatics."

"Sane men are labeled lunatics when they witness the impossible," Micah said. "These events never made it into history books because the solid evidence disappeared. It was simple to ignore the claims of the uneducated locals."

Chris shook his head. It was impossible. Except, he was sitting in a building that didn't exist yesterday.

Roberts said, "All this has made us better, as a species. These jumps forward in construction, they've all let us live in larger groups. Growing and storing food, walls to protect from marauders, and then the technology to live hundreds of feet above the ground, so we can fit even more of us. It's all been about bringing society together and moving us forward."

"And the men who've claimed these advancements for themselves have all become wildly successful," said Micah. "That's why we're here. Something in this building is new. It's waiting to propel society forward. And I want it. I won't make my ancestors' mistakes of giving the secrets away. I've built a construction empire for the sole purpose of being ready for this day. Whatever we find here, I can roll out rapidly. And it'll be mine."

Roberts looked uncomfortable. "But it will be an advancement. Sure, we'll get richer, but so will mankind."

"That's what you mean when you say 'purpose,'" Chris said. "What new advancement is hiding in here. Probably to let people live even more on top of each other."

"Exactly," Micah said.

Something else was bothering Chris. "That's a neat history lesson, but it doesn't explain all this. That dizzying room? Whatever took Dr. Terry? The open pit beneath the basement?"

"The pit confirmed that this building fit the pattern," Micah said. "Adjacent vacant spaces have been noted in each instance. In Vietnam, a cave in the mountainside never before noticed. In Idaho, they said it was a lava tunnel they'd never seen before. Your discovery of the pit beneath us made absolutely sure that this building was one of ours."

"Yours?"

"I told you, whatever we find in here belongs to me."

"Does your family library explain what the hell happened to Dr. Terry?"

"There are accounts from Sonora and Idaho of limping strangers. But no details. Nothing like what we witnessed in the hallway."

Chris thought of the lurching movement in the sub-basement and behind the frosted glass. A scared explorer might call that "limping."

"And nothing like that swirling craziness," Roberts said.

"So maybe that's your purpose," Chris said. "That's what's unique here."

"But what *is* it?" Roberts asked. "What's it doing? How does it help society like the other buildings?"

"We'll find more answers upstairs," Micah said. "I can feel it."

34

CHRIS'S CURIOSITY about Micah's motives was satiated.

And while what mysterious purpose this building might have was intriguing, it wasn't worth his life. Maybe if Eddie weren't in the picture, Chris could gamble on helping find the next leap forward in architecture and construction. A permanent gig with Micah's companies would be life-changing.

But something had burst from the wall and swallowed Dr. Terry.

Chris's top priority still had to be escaping to find Eddie.

The elevator moved again.

Micah stood next to the buttons, hands crossed over her waist.

Roberts stood over Chris. The blood-stained rag tied around his head made the giant bodyguard even more intimidating.

Chris could run once the doors opened, but that hadn't worked before. There hadn't even been any stairwells.

He could try jumping back into the elevator after they all got out. Unlikely that Roberts would let that happen.

No choice but to keep an eye open for another opportunity and stay as far away from walls as possible.

The upside was that Roberts seemed to be calming down from the stiff, angry man he'd met at the restaurant that morning. He was getting excited about helping mankind and those positive thoughts were making him more forgiving. Hell, Chris had just smashed open the man's head, and he didn't retaliate. That meant Chris could make further escape attempts without fear that Roberts would hurt him.

Micah, on the other hand—Chris was glad she'd only been carrying a taser. He had no doubt she would shoot him if he got in her way.

The elevator stopped at floor fifty, according to the LED numbers above the door. Judging from the height of the building outside, that meant they were only ten floors from the top. But from the buttons in the elevator and the directory they'd found in the courtyard, they weren't quite halfway up.

"How high do you think we are?" Chris asked. "The tower looks sixty stories maximum from the outside, but that says we've got seventy more to go." He pointed at the wall of numbered buttons.

Micah wrinkled her eyebrows.

Chris heartbeat picked up. He'd plucked her curiosity. "Let's find a window and see," he suggested.

Roberts eyed him suspiciously. "What's your play here?"

"It's not jumping out a fiftieth story window."

Micah shook her head. "We explore the floor. Find what we came here for. If we happen upon a window, then I'm as interested in the mystery as either of you. But it can't become the priority."

Chris felt hope seep away. He'd have to get them as far from the elevator as possible in another way.

Still, as the doors opened and they walked out into the lobby, Chris jammed a screwdriver into the door's latching mechanism. It should be quicker to open when he came sprinting back to it.

35

———

THIS LOBBY FACED a bare cinderblock wall.

Warmth emanated from the wall in front of them. Or from whatever was on the other side.

Hallways extended in either direction. They looked the same as the ones below.

Chris felt like he was repeating the same things, only last time it had ended with Dr. Terry getting swallowed by the building. There were only three of them left. Chris didn't like those odds.

As curious as he was about this building's purpose, he couldn't risk his life. Not when Eddie needed him.

If he couldn't run from or fight against Roberts, then he'd approach escape from another angle.

"That whole story you just shared made me think of something Leon and I saw in the sub-basements."

Roberts and Micah were peering down either hallway. Micah shrugged, motioned to the right, and Roberts gave Chris a gentle but firm shove. They were making him go first.

Fair enough, after his attack with the prybar, which Roberts now carried.

"Let's find a way into the center rooms," Micah said. "We may find our purpose there."

Chris kept his eyes straight ahead, his shoulders as far from the hallway walls as possible. He couldn't help but imagine what had happened to Dr. Terry. Was the old man wandering the floor beneath where he'd been swallowed? Were his molecules bonded with the tile? Had he been yanked away to wherever these buildings came from? Or was he eaten, digested for energy?

If Roberts was right that these overnight buildings were to benefit mankind, then how did he explain Dr. Terry and Leon? Were they the broken eggs necessary to make an omelet? The next step beyond indoor plumbing and air conditioning couldn't possibly be worth the lives of two men.

He pushed aside those thoughts. He needed to focus on getting back downstairs. "We didn't know what we were looking at down in the basement because you didn't tell us about the other buildings. If we'd known we were looking for some new purpose, we'd have paid more attention."

"What'd you see?" Roberts asked.

"At first, we thought it was HVAC units. Whatever you call the part that goes inside."

"The air handlers," Micah said.

"Yeah, that. But Leon pointed out they weren't vented to anything but the floor. And this was sub-basement three—nothing but that pit down below it."

"What do you think they were?" Roberts asked.

They rounded the corner. Ahead, orange light bathed the hallway, coming from glass doors to the center rooms.

Micah said, "Most likely, part of the HVAC system. If Chris doesn't know the name for air handlers, then we shouldn't trust him to recognize every existing model."

"I'm an architect, not a mechanical engineer." He shouldn't care about stupid insults when his life was in danger, but he did. "Leon didn't recognize them, either."

They approached the orange light. The temperature rose rapidly. Chris's cheeks and fingertips grew warm.

"A more efficient heating system?" Micah wondered to herself.

"I'm telling you, the answer may be downstairs." Chris walked deeper into the heat.

The glass doors came into view.

On the other side, a planetarium. Instead of a projection of stars, a blinding orange sun burnt in the center of the dome. Instead of theater seating, beach loungers.

"It's a giant tanning booth," Chris said.

Micah and Roberts caught up. Roberts peered around the room, searching for possible threats.

Micah squinted at the sun. "What's powering it?"

Chris wished he'd brought tinted glasses. The sun was its own smaller dome, inverted and extending downward from the peak of the planetarium ceiling. Its surface roiled, sunspots growing and shrinking, flares swinging out in burning loops.

"Is that our answer?" Roberts asked.

"It could be," Micah said. "Depending on where the power's coming from, how much it's using."

"As an architectural breakthrough, more efficient heating isn't really on par with the first steel structure," Chris said, "or indoor plumbing or air conditioning. Shouldn't we be looking for things we've never seen before?"

Roberts tapped on the glass. The mini-sun burned. "You've seen a lot of those?"

"I've seen heaters, yes." Chris motioned to the beach loungers. "And I've seen tanning booths. But neither me nor Leon had ever seen anything like those metal boxes downstairs."

"I want to get up there." Micah pointed to the sun. "I don't see any sort of attic access, do you?"

Roberts shook his head. "Maybe through the floor above?"

"That's what I was thinking."

Roberts turned Chris by his shoulders. "Lead the way."

Chris walked back toward the elevator lobby. He quickly found himself missing the warmth of the mini-sun. It was only November, but winter had come early, and he did much better in the warmer months. His problems always felt more conquerable in the sunlight.

"I'm telling you," he tried again, "the new thing is downstairs. We should check that out."

Frustration entered Roberts voice. "Give it a rest. You're a shitty con man. You're too obvious. We take the elevator to the basement, and you've got a maze to escape into, and plenty of stairwells to run back to the courtyard."

Chris bit down on his tongue. He was an idiot. He should have tried the deceptive approach before attempting to stab Roberts with a prybar.

"It's possible you're on to something with these metal boxes," Micah said, "but you've made clear that your primary intention is to leave. And so we'll investigate the sub basements with you, *after* we've explored these higher floors."

They reached the elevator lobby.

A tall figure hunched over the elevator door.

36

IN THE FLUORESCENT glow of the lobby's overhead lights, the thing hunching over the elevator door looked a pale yellowish bone color.

Chris could see the shape of a head and shoulders, but it was wearing a cloak or had wrapped itself in a blanket, and he couldn't tell where cloth ended and flesh began. Its legs were wrapped tightly together.

Chris backed into Roberts, who was just as frozen.

"What is it?" the big man whispered.

Micah shushed them.

It was like the thing was standing in shadow, difficult to see detail, except everything around it was in perfect view.

It hunched over, leaning close into the elevator doors. It pressed its face—or the area where its face should be—against the crack between doors.

A screwdriver fell out, bounced on the tile floor, and rolled to the center of the lobby.

The hunched figure turned toward Chris.

His heart dropped to his gut.

Still hunched so its face was hidden, its off-white covering —or loose flesh—raised and jolted with its movement. The thing lurched at them.

Chris leapt away, ready to flee, no longer worried about the hungry walls but about the lurcher, it had found him, caught up, and now it wanted him.

Roberts' iron grip closed around Chris's elbow.

Micah exhaled a noise between fear and pleasure.

The lurcher hopped and slid. Its bone color blurred to match the painted white cinderblocks behind it. The shiny elevator doors warbled as the thing moved.

And then it was gone. The patterns of its clothes or flesh disappeared into the patterns around it.

Chris's lungs burned. He gasped for air. He felt his pants to make sure he'd kept control of his bladder.

Having his understanding of the world attacked was one thing. A building going up overnight. A huge pit atop which the building floated. The shimmering surfaces of the bullpen, or the mini-sun of the planetarium. But none of those had been following him. None of them had lunged for him.

Through him.

"Is it invisible?" Roberts whispered. "It went all camouflaged there, didn't it?"

Chris grunted agreement.

Micah strode forward, waving her hand like checking for spiderwebs. "It's not here. It slipped away. Back to wherever this building came from."

"Some kind of angel," Roberts said to himself, but he didn't sound convinced.

That thing hadn't been a religious emblem to emulate, but something wrong and intrusive.

Micah picked up Chris's screwdriver. "Was this another poorly thought out scheme to run away?"

Chris only glared at her. She was supposed to be this world-changing billionaire, and here she was, threatening brute violence if he didn't play along in her attempts to claim more wealth and power. She'd just seen something impossible. Some creature, terrifying, but amazing. And she was still focused on Chris's role in her plan for more power.

"Don't convince yourself to hate me," Micah said. "Or cling to any fantasies that you'll run off, and then I'll be arrested and you'll be a hero. The only thing I might be charged with is trespassing. But considering no one owns this building, even that charge is unlikely."

"Your bruiser here won't let me leave. That's some kind of kidnapping charge."

"I owe you enough money to change your life forever. What would it take for you to drop those charges? Paying in cash instead of a check? Including a 'good faith' bonus?"

Chris realized she was right. If they all made it out of here alive, and she was still willing to pay, Chris would take the money and forget what she'd done. He had no choice. He couldn't afford a legal battle—not with Eddie depending on him.

He was ashamed to back down, but he had no other choice. He couldn't run. He couldn't fight. He couldn't trick them into letting him leave. He couldn't bully her with legal threats, even when she was clearly guilty.

The only way he was getting free and finding Eddie was to first help Micah find her answer.

"Alright, you win." He'd felt dejected before in his years-long job search. But complete defeat in this moment felt even worse. "Let's go upstairs. Maybe the wiring for that little sun is the next leap forward in construction. Let's avoid whatever the hell that lurcher was, though. I don't know why it cared about my screwdriver, but I'd rather learn as little about it as possible." He took his screwdriver back.

"Agreed," Micah said, "on all counts. Roberts, hold on to that prybar. I imagine we'll need it to tear up the floor to get to what we're after."

Chris walked back into the elevator, his own shoulders hunched over. He hoped Eddie had found his own way out. But now, if Chris made it out of here, after giving in to Micah's every demand, what kind of father would he be? Weak, dejected?

The doors slid shut. Chris could deal with that later. He needed to get free, and the only way to do that was to solve this mystery.

37

ONE FLOOR UP, the outer hallway now felt familiar.

Chris led the way between dull cinderblock walls, around the corner and to the glass doors to the center room. He walked briskly to avoid thinking about what might burst out of those walls to drag him away.

They reached the glass doors.

Inside was a cafe, everything white.

Ivory bar-height tables placed in a grid atop wood floors painted white. Globe light fixtures hung from the high ceiling. On one side of the room was a wall with doors that were marked as bathrooms with the stubby silhouettes of men wearing pants and women wearing skirts.

The mundaneness of the bathrooms struck Chris as out of place with the absurdity of what he'd seen below.

Roberts opened the door. Warm air drifted into the hallway. Likely a byproduct of the mini-sun below them. "Go on in to make sure it's safe."

"You're the bodyguard," Chris said.

"That's why he's staying out here with me," Micah said.

It didn't matter if he resisted. Roberts would throw him in, or Micah would convince him that he had no real choice.

Chris walked inside. With all the bright white, it was like a sci-fi doctor's office. Atop each pedestal table, a little porcelain bowl and a shot glass. The glasses held water. The bowls held two capsules each.

Chris walked to the bathroom doors. He prepped himself to sprint away if he found the lurcher on the other side. He pushed open the first door.

It was a bathroom. Toilet, sink, paper towels.

Chris laughed. In the building that appeared overnight, they'd stocked the paper towels.

He checked each bathroom to find the same thing.

There was nothing else to search in the room. He waved Micah and Roberts inside.

The two cautiously entered.

Roberts looked around, slack-jawed. "It's peaceful."

Micah scoped out the center of the room. She pushed a table aside. "The heat source should be under us, right here."

Roberts nodded but closed his eyes and inhaled.

Micah cleared her throat. The body guard exhaled and then joined his boss.

While they inspected the floor for a crack to insert the prybar, Chris fiddled with one of the capsules in the porcelain bowls. "If we're looking for a single purpose of this building, then what's up with the different floors? Trippy flashing lights, a mini-sun, now these pills?"

He popped open the capsule. Dried green plant fibers and minuscule beige beads. "These look like laxatives. I guess that makes sense with the bathrooms."

Roberts smashed the prybar into the floor. "Hey, do you have a hammer in your backpack?"

Chris took off the backpack, laid the rolls of blueprints on the table, and dug through the pockets until he found his claw hammer. The orange Home Depot sticker still stuck to the handle.

Micah held the prybar in between floorboards while Roberts swung the hammer. The sharp *clangs* echoed off the high ceiling.

"Seriously," Chris repeated, "what's up with all the different floors? All the other buildings you described had one new thing."

Roberts swung the hammer again. Wood splintered.

"Yes!" Micah cheered.

Chris touched the spilled powder to his tongue. Bitter. As far as he could tell, it was a laxative. Or at least a fiber supplement. And those little beige beads looked like probiotics. The purpose of this mysterious tower included regular, smooth bowel movements.

He chuckled at the thought. Sherri would call him immature for laughing at poop jokes. Eddie would be giggling hysterically.

Roberts heaved at the prybar. Wood cracked and a floorboard raised.

Pieces started to come together in Chris's mind. Pulsing colors and patterns, then warm sunlight, now a gut cleanse. It was all vaguely familiar.

Roberts worked the floorboard free and tossed it aside.

Micah shined a flashlight into the gap. "The heater should be right here. Where's the wiring?"

"Stand back," Roberts said. "I'll break through the next level."

It was a list of tasks that Chris was trying to remember, that the different floors were reminding him of. Not chores that Sherri had given him, but maybe something his therapist had once referenced?

Roberts swung the prybar like an ax.

Chris's mind churned.

Micah gasped, jerked around, then staggered backwards into Roberts.

Chris looked up.

Lurchers, their hunched, pale forms like bent-over men in head-to-toe straitjackets, pressed against the glass doors.

38

———

Chris scrambled for the doors opposite the approaching lurchers.

He found more of the things lunging through the glass. The glass stayed solid as the first passed through. In the same way that Chris's gaze couldn't focus on it, couldn't tell where cloth ended and flesh began, the glass didn't accept the lurcher's physicality, didn't notice that it should have shattered the pane.

Three more crossed through.

Chris stumbled back towards the bathrooms. Roberts and Micah followed, knocking aside tables with the prybar.

The lurchers' movement jerked. They moved faster than in the subbasement, or by the elevator.

The majority headed for the broken floor. Two locked onto Roberts and charged with their unearthly hopping and sliding.

Micah threw open a bathroom door and dashed inside.

Even in his panic, Chris refused to corner himself. He ran along the side wall toward the glass door to the hallway.

Roberts made himself into a barrier between the lurchers and Micah, blocking the door. The first lurcher fell forward and launched itself at Robert's knees. The bone-white, wrapped head—where a face would be if Chris could focus on it—*opened*. The covering lifted like a garage door. Finger-length tentacles wriggled forth.

Chris froze at the sight. He pressed himself harder back against the wall. The exit seemed impossibly far away.

Roberts swung the prybar. It connected with the diving lurcher's head. A tentacle was knocked loose. It skittered across the floor. The lurcher crashed into the wall, denting the drywall then dissipating through it.

Before Roberts could bring the prybar back up, the second lurcher, face lifted, tentacles exposed, latched onto his hand. Roberts screamed.

The big man's howl of terror and pain pierced Chris and broke him free of his paralysis. But if he ran again, he might draw the attention of the lurchers and those unnatural tentacles. He inched towards the exit, watching the lurchers that crouched over the damaged floor.

Roberts punched the attacking lurcher with multiple tight body blows. It sounded like punching a heavy bag and had as much effect. The thing's head enveloped his other hand. Dry, cracking tentacles felt their way up his wrist.

The lurcher ripped itself away. Roberts' hand hung limp, empty, and without the tips of three fingers.

Chris was halfway to the exit.

Roberts threw a wide punch at the lurcher, but it moved away and blurred against the white room until it vanished.

The lurchers hovering over the damaged floor swung around, one by one, to hop and slide out of view.

Where before the floor had been cracked and pried up, now it was returned to smooth, white wood.

Chris's chest heaved. This pristine room was as dangerous as any other. Nowhere in this building was safe. The walls closed in. The sterile lights grew blinding.

Roberts mumbled and inspected his fingers. They weren't bleeding, but Chris clearly saw they were missing after the last knuckle.

Micah emerged from the bathroom. Her reddish-gray hair was frazzled, and mascara smudged around her eyes.

Roberts stated the obvious. "They don't want us breaking anything."

Chris eyed the exit.

"Don't try it," Micah spat.

Roberts' head shot up, eyes narrowed. Even after losing body parts to an otherworldly creature, the man wielded his bulk like a sledgehammer.

The time to flee had passed. Chris had missed his shot.

39

THIS COULDN'T BE REAL.

Chris stayed pressed against the wall.

Architectural mysteries were one thing. It was another thing to see up close these monsters that appeared and disappeared, and magically repaired damage to the building, and lifted their faces like garage doors to set loose tentacles that dissolved fingertips.

Roberts inspected his shortened fingers. "I can't feel a thing in my hand."

Micah leaned on a table to catch her breath. "Did it inject you with an anesthetic?"

Their stoicism was infuriating. "Maybe it sucked away his nerve endings! How can you be so calm about this? We need to get out of here."

"We've been over this," Micah said evenly.

And they had. Chris had tried everything. He couldn't escape a man with Roberts' size and speed, and he couldn't convince Micah to leave. Until another opportunity came up, he was stuck.

But so was Micah's plan.

"You can't dig through the floor," Chris said. "So what now?"

"We continue upwards," Micah said.

Chris threw up his hands. "Until what?"

"Until we find the purpose of this building," Roberts said. "It's worth the risk for the good it might do."

Chris shook his head. "You keep saying that, but this building isn't like the others. There's no single new thing. It's a different mind-fuck on each floor."

"This must be how it looked," Micah said, "when they explored the original Tremont House in Idaho. The equipment on the ground floor, the ductwork through the walls, the frigid temperature even in summer. They were pieces of a whole."

"Then you tell me what great invention requires squiggly flashing colors on everything, and that mini sun, and now this gut cleanse." Chris picked up the laxative capsule for emphasis.

"I don't know," Micah said. "But the more we see of it, the clearer the answer will become."

Chris broke open the capsule. "I don't see anything special here. It looks like the green stuff in laxatives." He'd had a thought before the lurchers attacked, something about a discussion with his therapist. But adrenaline chased it away.

It would come back.

Micah sipped from a glass of water on the table. "This is just water. I don't know the purpose of this room. It may make sense once we see more of the picture."

Chris realized how thirsty he was and downed the glasses from three different tables. He'd been in here too long. He checked his phone. Still no service. "If you're insisting on risking our lives, let's get on with it, so I can get back to finding my boy."

They headed for the glass door they'd come through.

Through the glass partition with the hallway, Chris saw a small man walking in the shadows. He wore faded jeans and a dull camouflage jacket.

Leon.

40

EDDIE COULDN'T FIGURE out what he was seeing.

He and Cam had searched more offices, and now they'd just entered the twentieth floor. Twenty-first? Eddie wasn't sure. Everything was blending together.

The lights were all off.

Cam got out her phone and turned on the flashlight.

The wide beam of light fell on a toppled cubicle's walls. A crooked chair with broken wheels sat next to an upside-down desk.

"This don't make no sense," Cam whispered. "This is a brand new building. Someone already came in and smashed it up? And why'd they pick this floor?"

Eddie turned on his own flashlight app. The whole floor was smashed up. He didn't want to search here. Not in the dark. "Let's go to another floor. I don't know any hiding spots here. The game didn't have any rooms like this."

Eddie pointed his flashlight behind a cubicle wall that leaned on a desk. He didn't see anywhere to look, anyways.

He realized Cam hadn't responded. His gut sank. She'd

probably want to search this creepy place. And if he wanted her to stick around, he'd have to search it, too. He turned to look at her.

Her lips were tight and her eyes were wide. "What game?"

Eddie could tell she was mad, but he didn't know about what. "Treasure Hunter X. I play it with Chris."

Cam rubbed her forehead. "There's a skyscraper in this game?"

"Level three. I know all the hiding spots."

"Sixth floor, behind a painting." Cam's voice grew cold. "Ninth floor, in a floor-safe under a rug."

Eddie took a tentative step toward Cam. He wanted her to tussle his hair again so he'd know she still saw how helpful he was. "That's how I knew where to look. Me and Chris did it in the game."

Cam turned away. She pressed her forehead against the doorframe. She exhaled loudly.

Eddie's squeezed his hands closed. He wanted to hug her, even though she wasn't his old mom or Sherri or Chris or even all the way an adult.

She wasn't happy his hiding spots came from Treasure Hunter X. Hadn't he told her? He must not have.

The moths in his belly went crazy. This was worse than the strange man downstairs reaching across the room.

"I was trying to be helpful," he whispered. She'd said that didn't matter, and he'd almost believed her. But now that he wasn't helpful, she was angry.

When Cam pulled away from the doorframe, she looked as mad as Mom's old boyfriend. "A video game! What if we'd been in a car chase? Would you be throwing banana peels?"

Eddie bit his lip so it wouldn't quiver. He was too old to cry.

"This is real life, kid! That man down there wanted to hurt us."

"I'm sorry," Eddie choked out. "I thought I told you."

Cam's flashlight glistened in the tears that welled in Eddie's eyes. The creepy office went blurry.

Cam exhaled loudly again.

Eddie winced. "I'm not making excuses! I'm sorry."

Cam's face relaxed. "Excuses? Does somebody tell you to stop making excuses? This guy Chris?"

Eddie shook his head. "My mom."

"Your old mom. What would Chris say?"

Eddie shrugged. He wiped away snot with the back of his hadn't, then rubbed it on his jeans. "I don't know." He'd always been super helpful with Chris. But now that Chris was going to be Dad forever, Eddie didn't know how long he could keep it up. When Eddie made everything a cluster, what *would* Chris say?

Cam crouched down.

Eddie ran forward to hug her.

"Whoa." She went stiff, but Eddie squeezed her tighter until she hugged him back. "Okay. This is fine. But kid, what's with the waterworks? Didn't your old mom get mad at you? Sometimes people yell. It's not a big deal."

Eddie didn't know how to explain that after Mom got upset, she'd disappear inside her room for the rest of the day. Sometimes until tomorrow or the next day.

Eddie squeezed tighter.

"Okay, you little anaconda." Cam gently pushed away to look in his face. She wiped his tears with her sleeve. "You definitely forgot to tell me that the hiding spots were from a video game. I thought you said the man in your driveway told Chris about them."

He shook his head.

"But this man, he was real, right? Not from a video game?"

Eddie nodded. "They didn't know I was outside, but I listened the whole time."

"And he said there was treasure inside this building? Did he say the word 'treasure?'"

Eddie tried to remember exactly what the man had said. He knew that Chris was angry at the man. Angrier than Eddie had ever seen him. But he was sure of what he'd heard. "The man said that Chris couldn't keep staying in his house unless he found what's in here. I think he said money. Or maybe something worth a lot of money."

"Your new dad's behind on his rent?"

"I think Sherri makes more money, and she left."

"That sucks."

Eddie nodded. He didn't miss Sherri as much as Mom, but he did miss her.

Cam sat down. "Let's think for a minute."

Eddie pointed his flashlight around the dark open space. He tried not to imagine what might be hiding behind the smashed-up furniture.

"We've been looking in the wrong places. It's not about your video game. It's figuring out where someone would keep their valuables in an office building."

Eddie watched Cam think out loud. She hardly seemed to notice him.

"Maybe in a safe in the basement? But I'm not going down there again."

Eddie couldn't believe she wasn't still mad at him. She wasn't locking herself behind a door. Even though he hadn't been helpful. He'd been maybe the most unhelpful he'd even been—they'd been at this all morning, and they were doing it wrong because of him. But Cam wasn't angry anymore.

"You'd think there'd be safes in the biggest offices, where the rich managers work. But we didn't find any. So it's gotta be like one key location. Where do the richest people stay in a skyscraper?"

Eddie didn't get it. Adults wanted you to be helpful. If you blew it, then why would they need you around? Technically, Cam wasn't an adult yet. But Eddie didn't think that was the difference. When she turned eighteen, Cam wouldn't suddenly change her mind.

"If it were apartments, they'd stay in the penthouse. Is that the same for offices?"

Eddie guessed that Cam really did believe what she said earlier—that he didn't have to be helpful all the time. But even if it was true for Cam, that didn't mean it was true for other adults. It wasn't true for Mom. Definitely not for her old boyfriend. Except that didn't matter anymore.

The question now was whether Cam's theory was true for Chris. For Dad. Eddie would try to be helpful as long as he could, but at some point, he'd botch it. And then what would Chris do? Would he still want to be Dad?

So it didn't matter if Cam was right about some adults. Eddie couldn't risk it. He still had to be as helpful as possible. And right now, that meant finding the treasure - or the money, or whatever it was - to save Dad's house.

Cam paced in the dark. "I bet penthouses are a thing in office buildings, too. People want fancy views, even if they're at work, right? We gotta check the top floor. What do you think, Eddie?"

He nodded. The truth was, he didn't know where to look next. But Cam seemed confident. "I bet the treasure will be up there."

She pulled him to his feet. "That thing about security guards finding you in the elevator, that was in your game, right?"

Eddie nodded. He braced himself for her to get angry again.

"Perfect. We can take the elevator. Let's go find it." She looked around the dark room. "But let's go up one more floor first. Maybe the lights are on up there."

As Eddie followed Cam up the stairs, the thought came back of going deeper, even though they were headed up. And he liked it. Maybe this building was for him.

It wasn't empty or full. It was exactly what it was meant to be. And it was for him.

41

———

CHRIS WENT to throw the door open to ask Leon where he'd been.

Roberts' stumpy fingers closed like a vice around his shoulder.

"What's he doing?" Micah asked.

The sterile light of the central room partially reflected off the inside of the glass wall. Reflections of the white tables and walls interrupted the view of the dark hallway.

Chris recognized Leon's profile. There was no doubt it was the building-hacker-turned-building-inspector. But then Leon stepped behind a reflection.

Chris pulled against Roberts. "I want to know where he's been. Did he run off to save you from paying me?"

Micah's bemused shock answered that question. "I don't have time to plot my way around saving a few hundred thousand dollars. I have no idea where he's been. The only errand I sent him on was to help you find the blueprints."

Roberts hushed them both. "Look," he whispered.

Leon stepped back out from behind the reflection of a table. He leaned forward as he walked, like he was dragging something heavy or leaning into hurricane winds, but Chris couldn't see any physical impediment. Leon looked up, sniffed the air, and looked back over his shoulder.

He squeezed his eyes shut like a child watching a scary movie. He lowered his head. His body tensed hard enough that his neck quivered.

"What's he doing?" Micah whispered.

Roberts cupped a hand over her mouth. The large man held both Chris and Micah. He leaned against the glass to look up at the ceiling of the hallway. He shook his head and shrugged.

Finally, Leon opened his eyes to tentatively peer upwards. He silently gasped, dropped to the floor and covered his head. He rocked again like a child after a nightmare.

"What's that sound?" Roberts whispered, barely audible.

Chris didn't hear anything. Not even Leon's obvious whimpering. But the closer he looked at Leon, the more seemed wrong. Scratches covered his fingers that now clenched the back of his head. Maybe it was the shadows, but his skin looked gray, and not from the dust that was smeared all over him.

"He needs help," Chris said.

Roberts snapped a hand over Chris's mouth. "Can't you hear that?"

Micah pried Roberts' hand from her face. "Do not treat me like a child," she hissed. "What are you claiming to hear?"

Roberts pushed her behind him. "I'm in charge until it's safe again."

Micah exhaled in frustration.

Chris pulled against Roberts, trying to see down the hallway. It was empty, as far as he could see.

Leon jerked three feet backwards. His face dragged on the tile floor, leaving a smear of blood. Keeping his face down, he crawled to his knees and inched forward again. He still strained like he was dragging something.

Chris couldn't leave him out there. He bit down on Roberts' damaged fingers.

No reaction.

He still had no feeling.

Chris moved just enough to free his mouth. He shouted, "Leon, we're in here!"

Leon's head snapped up. Eyes wide with hope, he looked right at Chris. Through Chris.

Roberts growled. He shoved Chris to the side and braced himself against the glass door.

Chris's shoulder absorbed the impact with the cold floor. He jumped to his feet, ignoring the pain. "Let him in. There's something wrong out there."

"That's why he's staying where he is."

Leon turned to crawl towards the inner room. Whatever he'd been dragging down the hallway now seemed to rotate with him. He still strained with each movement.

Roberts winced and covered his ears. "How can you stand that noise?"

Micah had circled around to watch Leon from the side. "What noise?"

"It sounds like a dial-up modem in a bowl of jello. You don't hear it?"

Leon crawled closer to the door, almost in arms' reach now.

"Let him in!" Chris yelled again. He tackled Roberts' knees. Pain throbbed in his shoulder. The bodyguard barely flinched from the impact.

"He may have information to share," Micah said.

On the floor by the glass door that Roberts held shut, Chris was now at eye level with Leon.

Down the hallway, high above where the ceiling should have been, something shifted in the darkness. Something massive, larger than the tower.

Then Leon reached the glass. Blood dripped out of his nose. Tears smeared the dust on his cheeks. It was green. Leon locked eyes with Chris, finally seeing him. He reached for the glass between them.

Roberts stomped down between Chris and the glass, then shoved him backwards.

It saved Chris's life.

Leon's hand didn't stop at the glass. Like it had done for the lurchers, the glass simply forgot that it should either hold stable or shatter. Instead, Leon's hand reached through like a projection.

In the white light of this central room, the discoloring of Leon's skin was more evident. It was gray as a toad's flesh and unevenly coated in a green dust that reminded Chris of powdered candy.

Leon's arm followed, then his shoulder, and finally his face.

As his mouth appeared, his cries suddenly became audible.

His scream contained terror, pain, and hope. He moved his mouth and worked his tongue, but only gibberish came out.

Chris reached for him to drag him the rest of the way through.

Roberts kicked at Chris to keep him away. Only Chris's little finger touched Leon's hand.

Raw pain flooded into Chris's finger.

42

THE WORLD REGRESSED to bright light and searing pain.

Where the light was omnipresent, the pain pulsed in rapid-fire tidal waves from the little finger of Chris's right hand.

Leon's panicked face pierced the white light. He threw his head from side to side. Gusts of agony timed to Leon's movement.

Leon's screams had bisected, taken on a second part.

Adrenaline kicked in.

Chris lurched backwards but his finger was jammed inside something. The attempt made the pain overwhelm his survival instincts. He tried to curl into a ball.

Suddenly, a face pressed against his. Micah cooed to him. "Let go. Relax your hand."

Something crashed. Roberts cursed. "He's still coming. Pull Chris back."

Thin arms under Chris's shoulders. Wiry fingers clasped across his chest.

The comforting whispers cleared Chris's head enough for him to look around.

Leon held tight to Chris's finger. The small man crawled toward him as Micah dragged him away.

Roberts knocked over a table onto Leon, who ignored it.

Leon reached for Chris's face with his other hand. Pale, gray fingertips filled Chris's vision.

A table leg knocked Leon's hand away.

"Keep pulling him," Roberts yelled, then moaned, "I'm sorry."

A slight scrape of metal on metal, a glint of steel. Roberts grabbed Chris's hand.

"No!" Micah yelled.

"Look at it!" Roberts cried.

Through the pain, Chris looked at his hand.

His little finger shared the space with Leon's index finger.

Starting at the second knuckle, his finger merged with Leon's. Chris's skin, red from exertion, speckled Leon's gray flesh. Chris's fingernail was buried somewhere beneath that sickly color. The tip of Leon's finger extended out from Chris's finger below the knuckle, at a downward angle.

Panic prompted flailing, which closed Chris down to everything but the pain.

"Do it!" Micah shouted in his ear.

Chris felt his hand smash against the tile. A second flavor of pain torrented into his finger, sawing, clawing.

His arm whipped free. He fell backwards. Micah grunted as she absorbed his fall.

Then Chris was in the air, bouncing away from the crawling gray man. Drops of blood floated in Chris's wake, splattering Micah's shirt as she followed.

43

ADRENALINE AGAIN WON the battle against pain. It was easier now that the pain had subsided to mere agony.

Chris wriggled down from Roberts' shoulder.

They ran down the hallway, opposite the side they'd entered the white room.

Roberts' bulk took up Chris's view ahead. Behind him, Micah ran, watching back over her shoulder.

Behind her, sterile light through glass walls illuminated the cinderblock and tile hallway.

Leon howled haunting gibberish that may have included the word, "help."

Something wet dripped down Chris's hand and wrist.

He looked down as he ran. His little finger was gone. All that remained was a tatter of flesh and sinew, where Roberts must have given up on cutting and torn the rest off.

Micah handed him a handkerchief. "Don't bleed out. We won't carry you."

Chris wrapped it around the stub and held it tight. "I can't tie it myself."

"We get to safety first," Roberts said.

Chris applied pressure to where his finger should have been. He knew there'd be consequences from this. Everyday life made more difficult. But right now, he wanted to get as far away as possible from the pain he'd felt before Roberts cut him free.

They reached the corner of the hallway. Roberts waved them to a stop. He peeked around the corner. "Looks clear. Stay away from the walls."

They hurried to the elevators.

Micah pressed the up button. It glowed.

"No." Roberts pressed the down button, but the up button stayed lit. "This is too dangerous now."

"I'm in charge," Micah said.

"I keep you safe. I'm taking you back down. I'll return with a trained team."

Micah tied off Chris's handkerchief. "I hired you because you're the best. You'll keep me safe because I'm paying you a fortune to keep me safe. Do you need a whole team to do your job?"

Chris winced at the pain.

"I'll find the gift from the other side and bring it to you," Roberts said. "After you're outside the building. The architect is right. This isn't like the others."

"Don't doubt the work," Micah said. "We've seen the same overnight appearance, the same nearby open space. The answer is here."

A howl from up the hallway. Leon was still following them.

"I have to find Eddie." Chris's purpose came back through the pain. "He can't be in here."

"We're in over our heads," Roberts said.

"Don't be selfish," Micah said. "What about the good you want to do? We'll make the world a better place."

Roberts exhaled.

A second howl, from the other direction.

They all turned to look down the hallway. In the far corner, shadows moved as someone drew near.

Two elevators dinged. One up-arrow illuminated, and one down-arrow.

The up elevator opened first.

"We're not done yet," Micah said.

Chris squeezed shut his eyes. He resisted the urge to lay down and sob until Leon caught him. Then he realized Micah couldn't keep him here. Roberts was the physical threat, and he was no longer convinced. "I'm going home."

He stepped in front of the other elevator. The down arrow glowed like a lighthouse in a storm.

The doors opened.

A black horizon in the distance. Rocks and dirt, low crumbling walls coated in green dust.

Dr. Terry crouched next to a stone wall.

Reality shifted, and Dr. Terry was squatting in a plain elevator car.

He made the motions of shelving books, but his hands were empty. He patted the ground next to him, not looking until he found his invisible target. He picked it up, and then carefully turned his head to look, slowly opening one eye like a child afraid of a jack-in-the-box. Whatever he saw wasn't what scared him. His shoulders relaxed, and he shelved his invisible book.

Chris backed away.

Leon howled again.

Dr. Terry's head whipped around. His wrinkled cheeks were now gray. His tweed blazer hung in tatters, and his beard and mustache were caked with green. He locked hollow eyes with Chris.

His mouth opened, and a tired wail came out. His words slurred but were more intelligible than Leon's. "You can still help me! The temperature hasn't dropped yet!"

Chris wanted to run. There were elevators on the opposite side of the building. There had to be stairs somewhere.

Leon screamed, turned the corner. He dragged himself by his arms.

Another howl from the other direction. Another gray man. Chris thought he recognized him as the man who'd yelled down from the skybridge in the courtyard. That felt like ages ago.

Micah tugged Roberts toward the empty elevator with the up arrow illuminated. "It's the only option now."

Dr. Terry shook his head. "Don't leave." He patted the wall where he'd been shelving something. "It's not that bad. Most are blank. They require almost nothing."

The old professor took an awkward step towards Chris.

Chris's finger throbbed, the pain a fraction of what he'd felt before.

He fled into the empty elevator. Roberts and Micah entered close behind.

Chris mashed the "close doors" button. As the doors slid shut, Dr. Terry hobbled into view.

Chris pressed the "L" button, and far above, a motor kicked on.

Downward pressure on his body as the elevator headed upwards.

"Why won't it go down?"

Roberts pointed to the bank of floor buttons, and for the first time, Chris saw fear in the large man's expression.

The topmost button was lit up. *120.*

"Who pushed that?" Chris demanded.

"You'd have seen if we did it," Micah said. "Someone called it up."

44

THE LED NUMBERS above the door ticked upwards.

Chris mashed the STOP button.

The elevator continued. The motor above thrummed.

The glowing button labeled "120" taunted him. He tried pressing other floors, to at least give them a chance to get off, but no other buttons lit up.

"We have to get back down," Chris said.

"Don't interfere," Micah ordered. Her blouse was wrinkled and splattered with Chris's blood, but her expression remained resolute. "We're going to the top and finding answers."

The LED numbers ticked past 40.

Chris looked to Roberts for support. The bodyguard avoided eye contact with Micah and tried the STOP button. It still didn't work. "We can't use what's in here to change the world if we're dead. You can't get richer if you're dead."

"This isn't about money," Micah said.

"Money, power, your face on Time Magazine, what's the difference?" Chris reached his left hand into his backpack, fishing for a screwdriver. "It won't protect you from Leon and Dr. Terry."

"Or what happened to them," Roberts added. He felt around the panel that housed the floor buttons.

Micah stomped her foot. "You won't stop this elevator."

Chris found his screwdriver and handed it to Roberts. "How do we protect ourselves from them? The lurching things don't want us to damage the building. Fine, we won't pry up any more floors. But Leon wanted our help." Chris saw Leon's pleading face, his desperation to escape from whatever he was dragging. "We should try to help them."

"You touched him and cried like a stuck pig," Roberts said. "We're not in a position to rescue anybody." He worked the screws that held in the button panel.

The LED numbers ticked passed 60.

The elevator rattled. Chris felt a hum in his feet that worked its way up his bones.

"If you leave now," Micah said, "you'll be abandoning them."

Chris felt like a coward, but Roberts was right. He couldn't rescue them when he didn't understand what was happening to them, and taking the time to understand would risk that extreme pain again.

Or what would have happened if Leon had kept crawling over him? Would they have meshed fully? Maybe Leon was dragging others who'd tried to rescue him.

Chris dug his fingers under the loosened panel to yank it off. It came free, exposing buttons and wires.

Roberts fumbled behind the STOP button. "The wiring's loose. Depressing it doesn't complete the circuit. But if I hold this like... there, hit the button."

Chris pressed it.

The elevator continued.

Micah scoffed. "You're not stopping it. We're going to see what's at the top."

"Try the same thing with the next floor."

The LED lights approached 80.

"Fix the wiring for 85."

Roberts felt behind the buttons. "Good call. All the wiring's loose back here." He stretched and reached and then hit the button.

"85" glowed yellow.

The elevator slowed.

Micah lunged for the buttons. Roberts held her back.

As Chris held his throbbing hand, he remembered, "The building was only 60 stories. Where are we?"

The doors opened to the 85th floor.

45

———

THIS TIME, the glass doors to the interior space were right in front of the elevators.

Which was helpful, because the outer hallways extended at least two hundred yards before they curved out of sight.

"You see that, right?" Chris asked.

Roberts shook his head. "That's not possible. The building took up less than a block."

Micah whispered to herself as she peered down the hallways.

"Anything like this in your family history books?" Chris asked.

"This could be the breakthrough," Micah said. "Fitting more space inside a building. The last three breakthroughs were about extending living and working space upwards. Now we're expanding in new directions."

Chris shook his head. "The other weirdness has been in the center rooms. This hallway trick feels more like a side effect."

"Now you're offering your opinion?"

"My opinion is we should leave. We try the other elevator, or we find a stairwell."

"What about the building's purpose? What about in there?" Micah pointed through the glass.

Chris realized he'd been avoiding even looking inside.

The central room was dark, lit only by purple neon. A freestanding staircase rose twenty feet, and then a smooth, curved ramp led back down. The edges were lined with pulsing purple neon.

There were three similar structures in the room, each higher than the last. The tallest stood at least fifty feet high. Chris couldn't see the ceiling.

"That light is moving at the same pace as the swirly stuff in the LSD room," Roberts.

He was right. The lights brightened and dimmed in steady waves.

He'd seen something similar before but still couldn't remember where.

It didn't matter because those staircases didn't go down. The exit wasn't in there.

Chris tried the second elevator in the lobby. He pressed the down button, and it lit up, but the elevator didn't respond. "Roberts, try your hotwiring trick again."

Roberts inspected the panel. "I can't. There's no exposed screws. We'd have to pry it off."

The thought of the lurchers finding them again made Chris shiver. Or maybe that was the blood loss. He squeezed his hand. It had clotted so he was okay for now, if a little light-headed. "Alright, then we find a stairwell." He started down the stretched-out hallway.

"Is this the best idea?" Roberts asked, walking behind.

Micah quickly caught up to walk by Chris's side. "We're looking for the mechanism that allows this spatial extension."

"Yeah," Chris said, "either that or stairs down so we can get the hell out of here."

Micah pursed her lips.

They walked briskly between cinderblock walls. Chris cradled his hand against his gut. The relief that he'd felt at escaping that extreme pain was fading as the constant ache of his missing finger persisted.

They found no corners, but after twenty minutes of a gentle curve, they reached another lobby. Elevators to the left, the central room to the right.

Neither elevator responded to the buttons.

Chris continued on. Another twenty minutes and they returned to where they started. One elevator remained open.

"Now what?" Roberts asked.

"We go up a floor at a time," Chris said, "until we find a way back down." He couldn't think too closely about it, or panic welled in his chest. It wasn't Micah or Roberts keeping him inside now—it was the building itself.

He stared at the purple neon through the glass. The pulsing was relaxing in a deep, subtle way.

"These buildings want to be found out," Micah said. "I suspect the way back down will reveal itself once we've discovered what we're meant to know."

"In the others," Chris asked, "were there any reports of people getting trapped inside?"

Micah avoided eye contact. "No. But as you've pointed out, those discoveries were much simpler. It's possible those men never had a chance to realize they were being kept inside before they found the building's purpose."

"Bullshit," Roberts said. "If I didn't know you, I'd think you were losing your mind. I almost wish you did have some brain imbalance because the alternative is that you're more obsessed than I realized."

Micah responded with venomous fury, but Chris's mind had spiraled down a rabbit hole, chasing a thought triggered by Roberts' anger.

Brain imbalance.

Ideas fell into place, but he had to be sure.

He opened the glass door and walked into the dark room.

Roberts called, "Hey!" and then the door shut between them.

A high-pressure silence pressed inside Chris's ears. In the dark, purple neon pulsed in a calming rhythm. He picked the highest platform and hurried up the stairs. His thighs ached. He felt his heartbeat in the nub of his missing finger.

The top felt impossibly high, far higher than the fifty feet it'd appeared from below. Micah and Roberts' flashlights were pinpricks below him.

He wasn't sure what to expect. He took a tentative step onto the ramp that curved downwards, between two strips of pulsing purple.

Frictionless, the floor yanked him to his rear. He plummeted down the slide. Air rushed past his ears and the chilly barrage forced his eyes closed. His skin pressed upwards, his thighs pressed up into his hips, and his gut pushed heavy into his chest. He held his hands across his stomach until the raw force of the fall flung them above his head.

Still he fell, sliding down the smooth ramp, until the shock faded and he was only in this moment, the rare, exhilarating sensation of free fall, faster than terminal velocity.

He forced his eyes open. Purple neon tubes banded the edges of the ramp, but otherwise there was no protection from falling. Chris didn't know what kept him at the center of the ramp, only that if he slid off, he'd plummet straight down to the solid floor below.

It reminded him of the first time he'd ridden a jetski at age 11. His dad had ignored the rental company and allowed Chris to ride on his own, chasing his parents' pontoon boat. Barely in control of the machine, he'd decided to jump his parents' wake. With only ninety-seven pounds to weigh it down, the jetski had flown above the waves. That loss of control had terrified him, but as he landed, bounced, then managed to keep hold of the handles, he'd felt amazing.

That same adrenaline surged through him now.

The slide spat him out on the ground floor.

Roberts stood over him. "What the hell was that?"

Micah's neck stretched backwards to look up at the slides.

"I think I know what this is," Chris said. "But I'm not sure yet. Let's go up one more floor."

They returned to the elevator, and once Roberts rigged the wires to light up the button for 86, they all got on.

Floor 86 had similarly extended hallways to floor 85. Chris ran up to the glass doors to look into the central room.

The whole floor was a treadmill.

"That's it. I don't get it, but that's what this is."

"Quit playing coy," Micah said. "What do you think you've discovered?"

Chris thought of where to begin.

Years ago, during the first session of therapy for his anxiety, his therapist had given him a faded photocopy of a brochure. She dipped into a rehearsed explanation.

"Anxiety and depression are physical ailments. We're talking about chemical imbalances in your brain. You're either creating too little dopamine and serotonin, or they're not getting to where they need to be. But I promise this is good news. In addition to our sessions where we'll talk through specific worries and learn positive self-talk, I also want you to pick three of these items to focus on. Think of them as physical therapy for your brain. Just like stretching or small exercises can help muscles heal, these activities can help your brain heal. They've each been shown to help the production or absorption of serotonin or dopamine."

The photocopy had a bulleted list.

Journaling

Exercise

Meditation

Sunlight

Eating fewer processed foods

Visiting friends

It went on for three columns of mundane activities that this university or that research center had found to balance dopamine and/or serotonin.

As Micah and Roberts watched expectantly, Chris thought of what he'd seen in the building so far.

Wavering colors that pulsed like meditation video aids.

A miniature sun that sure as hell felt like real sunlight.

A gut cleanse.

And hadn't he felt calmer in the rooms? He'd seen Dr. Terry immediately relax and reevaluate himself.

They didn't all add up—the pulsing surfaces weren't like the binaural beats videos he'd found to help with meditation

—but it was possible the builders knew more about manipulating the human brain than current psychologists.

There was a thought he hadn't considered since earlier this morning.

The builders.

Micah spoke through calmly clenched teeth. "What's the purpose of this tower?"

Chris said it out loud. "The peak of architectural psychology. It's psychotherapy packed into a box."

Roberts whispered in awe. "That's why it brought us all together in cities."

Chris nodded. "To fix our brains."

46

———

"Is that enough, Micah?" Chris asked.

As they stood in the elevator lobby of the tower's 86th floor, between two hallways that extended farther than was physically possible, outside a gymnasium-sized room with a floor that was one big treadmill, Chris couldn't believe that he'd fanboyed over this selfish, stubborn woman only a few hours ago.

Micah leaned on the glass doors, eyes closed. Her lips moved silently.

Chris looked to Roberts, who held up a finger. Give her a second.

Chris was out of seconds. "That's your answer. Everything in here is designed to fix neurotransmitters. An hour a day in here, and I bet anyone with anxiety or depression would pop out cured." He realized he believed that this building could cure his lifelong anxiety. But instead of relief or hope, it made him uneasy. This building was not benevolent. He'd spent years managing his problems. Just switching it off felt unnatural.

"No, no, no," Micah whispered. "Glass panes, iron frames, air conditioning designs, indoor plumbing. It's *one* breakthrough at a time. I'm going to take the next *one* breakthrough and apply it universally. I can't put these mental obstacle courses inside every residential and commercial building."

"It's still amazing," Roberts said. "Think of how many people we'd help with a building like this in every major city. Several thousand people a day could go through. We could end mental illness."

That thought sent a shiver through Chris. Eddie in here was bad enough. But thousands of people, in hundreds of cities, every single day. Better to trudge through therapy than risk whatever this building was.

"There are a hundred twenty floors of this," Micah said. "How much time and money to reverse engineer each of them? To develop the technology and build it?"

"So we start with a dozen or so floors," Roberts said.

"Regardless," Chris raised his voice. "There's your answer. Both your answers, actually. How was it built? Underground, and then lifted up."

"We don't know that," Micah said.

Chris ignored her. "Why was it built? To end mental illness. I've done my part. I'll take that check now, and then I'm finding my son."

"How do you intend to leave?" Micah asked. "The elevator only goes up."

"Roberts fixed the wiring for these two floors. He'll fix the button for the courtyard."

Roberts shrugged. "It could work. But what about Leon and Dr. Terry?"

Chris shoved down his guilt. "I'm not a cop. Or a scientist, or a priest, or whatever it would take to help them. I'll help the authorities however I can to rescue them once I've got Eddie outside."

Roberts waved him off. "Not that. Of course we'll help them if we can, but..." he pointed at Chris's missing little finger. "What I mean is, why did the building take them? What does that have to do with fixing mental illness?"

Chris hung his head. This was too much. His explanation of the tower's purpose didn't answer most of the more pressing questions. How was it lifted out of the ground? What were the lurchers? What had taken Leon and Dr. Terry, and where did it take them?

And most pressing of all, how could they leave?

"Let's ponder the tower's motivations once we're outside," Chris said.

He led the way back to the elevator.

"We have to see what's on the top floor," Micah said. The button for the hundred-twentieth floor still glowed.

"This building wasn't that tall," Chris said. "Not from the outside, anyways. I don't want to know what's up there."

Roberts reached behind the button panel. "There. Did that work?"

None of the other buttons lit up. Chris tried the bottom floor buttons anyways. Nothing.

Micah lunged for the button panel. Roberts caught her and walked her back to the corner of the elevator.

"You're fired," she yelled.

"We'll chat about that outside," Roberts said. "Here's what I'm thinking. Chris, you kept talking about what the building looked like outside. Well, I saw windows from the roof to the ground. And I haven't seen a single window in here. What's that tell us?"

"Space is acting weird," Chris said. "Like the hallways being too long and suddenly round."

"No, you gotta bend time and space to get that answer," Roberts said.

"And that's an issue? Have you not noticed the lurchers appearing and disappearing? Or Leon and Dr. Terry half out of our dimension? His finger got stuck in mine!" Chris held up his four-fingered hand. "I think we're pretty far into bending space."

"The simpler answer," Roberts continued on, as unstoppable in reasoning as he was physically, "is that these outer hallways aren't the outer*most* hallways, know what I mean?"

Chris pictured the ground floor. He and Leon had entered through a vestibule between the outer doors and the courtyard. He tried to remember how deep that had been. Leon had stopped to look into a vent, and there'd been plenty of space between them and the doors on either side. At least ten feet both ways.

The elevator banks were all inside the courtyard, twenty or more feet from the outer walls.

So Roberts had a point.

"Maybe there's stairs in that direction." Chris pointed to the back of the elevator.

"A useless proposition," Micah said. "We haven't seen any doors on the outer walls of the hallways. And if we tried to force our way through, those things you call *lurchers* would return."

"If we got through quickly enough," Roberts said, "they'd probably ignore us to fix the wall."

Chris thought of what Leon had said down in the basement when he'd been excited to start building hacking again. "There's always a way through." He pointed at the ceiling of the elevator.

There was a hatch.

47

———

THE ELEVATOR SHAFT was a vertical wind tunnel.

Chris dropped his backpack, put his flashlight in his teeth, and climbed Roberts' shoulders to reach the top of the elevator car.

A steady downward draft whipped his hair about and cooled his scalp.

He clicked on his flashlight. The walls were dull steel. The elevator rode tracks on either side of the shaft. A pulley system of steel cords hooked to the elevator and disappeared up into the darkness.

Chris leaned over the bright square of the open hatch. "What if we unhooked the cable? There should be brakes to stop us at the bottom, right?"

Micah laughed.

"It hasn't come to that yet," Roberts said. "I don't trust this building to have those failsafes."

It was an extreme idea, but Chris wasn't totally convinced it was the wrong one.

He went back to inspecting his surroundings.

Above, every fifteen feet were sliding double doors. The flashlight illuminated five of them before the dark took over.

Chris turned around.

For every set of doors that led to an inner floor, another set of doors was on the opposite side of the shaft, facing the outer edge of the building.

"I'll be damned," Chris said. "Roberts, you were right!"

Roberts pulled himself up to stick his head through the hatch. "I should have realized it earlier. But this will be easier than I thought."

High above, the elevator motor kicked on. The steel cable creaked. The elevator started moving up.

Roberts cursed and dropped back down.

The elevator was flush with front and back walls, but to the sides, there was a gap wide enough to fall through. The car's movement quickly made Chris aware of the unevenness of the roof. It was pitched toward the drop-off.

Chris clung to the cable, focused on not looking at the gap.

He moved for the open hatch but then hesitated. If Roberts couldn't get it stopped again, they'd go straight to the top.

This tower was not benevolent.

Chris didn't want to know what was up there.

As they passed the next floor, Chris got a close look at the doors on the outer wall of the shaft. A tiny sliver of light shone through the center. Sunlight.

Hope sprung to life.

The elevator gained momentum.

In a few moments, the elevator would be moving too quickly for Chris to do anything but crawl back below.

He had no time to mull over a decision, so he acted.

At the next floor, he threw himself at the outer door. He pressed his cheek and his gut against the cold metal. The sunlight from the other side shined directly in his eye.

The elevator car scraped his heels. There wasn't enough space.

He jammed his fingers between the doors. The elevator crushed his leg against the outer door. Muscles stretched. The top corner of the car caught his buttocks and lifted him.

His head hit the top of the doorframe. The elevator kept moving. His neck turned at an unnatural angle. Nerves protested. His shoulder touched the top of the doorframe, and he felt his spine compressing.

His pants ripped. The top corner of the car moved past his buttocks to scrape his back, his neck, his ear. Then he was squeezed in between the doors of the car, and the doors of the shaft. The six inches felt like a ballroom.

He jammed his fingers back in between the doors.

The bottom edge of the car moved up. It'd be one more crushing moment and then an open drop into the chasm below the tower.

The doors inched open.

The bottom edge of the car brought his knees up to his waist.

Chris worked his flashlight between the doors to pry them open.

The bottom edge of the car pushed up past his ankles.

No time left. He yanked on the flashlight as hard he could. The doors opened four inches.

Chris reached in, forced his shoulder through the gap, widening it another inch.

The elevator car squeezed his calves, his knees, his thighs.

He wriggled against the doors. His ear pressed against the cold metal.

The car squeezed his hips but moved past without forcing him upwards.

Empty air felt cool on his scratched legs.

He jackknifed his elbow to bring his hand back around and grip the doors. He pushed. Another five inches, enough to get his head through.

The elevator car passed by. Then metal screeched above, and the car stopped.

Chris dangled over the open elevator shaft. The steady downward draft became a pressurized burst as the air squeezed past the elevator car. Chris swung his other arm around, grabbed the doors, and pulled himself up.

He collapsed onto a cold floor.

His legs stung. He thought he was bleeding on his upper thigh. His ear was numb. He'd strained a muscle in his neck. But he could move. Nothing broken.

Except his flashlight. It wouldn't click on.

Not that it needed to. Sunlight filtered through gray clouds poured through a wall of windows.

Chris sat up and looked around.

48

———

Eddie and Cam didn't find an elevator the next floor up.

Not on the one after that, either.

In fact, the next eight floors were dark, trashed offices.

In the ninth trashed office, they found a water cooler on its side. After Cam sniffed it and tasted it, they gulped it down.

It was the best tasting drink Eddie'd ever had. That solved his being thirsty, but he was pretty sure lunch would have been over an hour ago. His stomach growled.

They kept climbing.

"Two weird things I noticed," Cam said between sharp breaths. "First, where the hell's the windows? Second, don't these offices seem smaller than the building looked outside?"

Eddie wasn't sure.

"I mean, this building is most of a block. The offices aren't a quarter that size."

That made sense to Eddie. "So, what's that mean?"

"I don't know if we're seeing the whole floor."

They reached the next landing—another dark, trashed office.

"You want to explore inside?" Eddie asked, hoping she'd say no.

"Thing is, there's no windows in there. These offices must be on the inside. I think we're missing something on the outside. Problem is, the only doors out of this stairwell face into these offices."

"In Treasure Hunter X, after the office building level, it's a haunted mansion. The treasure's in the attic."

Cam raised her eyebrow, but Eddie talked faster.

"There's a bunch of ways upstairs. A secret tunnel, stairs, a ladder, a dumbwaiter. They don't connect to each other. But they all connect to the big room in the attic."

"Ah, I get it. We can't get to the elevator from the stairs, but maybe we can from in there." She pointed her flashlight into the office.

Eddie's gut twisted. He'd rushed to share a helpful idea, and now he'd given them the perfect reason to explore the dark office.

He peeked through the door. The little flashlight revealed a row of flipped desks and busted chairs. A cubicle wall had fallen onto a potted plant, shattering the fake clay and spilling real dirt onto the carpet.

Cam took his hand. Her fingers were warm. "We'll follow the wall around. If there's no elevators, then we'll search the middle of the room."

Halfway around, they found a tall bookshelf had fallen through the wall. No boards or metal to hold it up - it was just drywall.

"What kind of shitty construction?" Cam stepped around the shelf.

Curiosity got the better of Eddie. He poked his phone's flashlight and his head through the hole.

The space was like an empty closet, except as big as a basketball court. With the short reach of his light, he couldn't be sure the far wall was blank.

"We should check in here," he said.

Cam stuck her head in beside him. Her hair tickled his cheek. "Reminds me of my high school's old gym, but less dusty."

They dragged the bookshelf back and stepped through the hole.

The floor looked to be the same drywall material as the walls. As thin as the walls were, Eddie stepped carefully. It held firm.

"Looks empty," Cam said.

They walked towards the end of the room, flashlights up.

The far wall was bare. The only interruption in the empty room was the hole where the shelf had fallen.

"No luck." Cam patted Eddie's back. "But I wonder..."

She kicked the wall. Her foot went through the drywall.

Together, she and Eddie peeled back the crumbly wall. This section had skinny steel beams holding up the drywall. And on the other side, a flat metal sheet.

Eddie touched it. It chilled his fingers. "I think this is the outside wall."

"But it was windows everywhere," Cam said. "Do they put fake windows on skyscrapers?"

Eddie shrugged.

Cam kicked another hole in the wall, ten feet away. They

peeled back more drywall to find more steel studs and blank metal sheets.

Cam's shoulders drooped. "Nothing. Let's head back."

Eddie's cell phone dinged.

A flurry of text messages appeared, all from Dad.

"We must have finally got service this close to the outside," Cam said, checking her own phone.

Eddie read his texts. His heart sank. "He told me not to come. He sounds angry."

"Easy there," said Cam. "Remember, people get angry and yell, and it don't mean nothing. Sometimes, families gotta yell at each other. Work things out."

Eddie nodded. When Mom and her old boyfriend yelled, it wasn't to work things out. It made things worse. But Eddie liked Cam's ideas. And Chris was more like Cam than he was like Mom.

He kept reading the texts. "He said he was coming to find me. Then he texted when he got here to say to come outside."

"Think he's still out there?" Cam asked.

Eddie shook his head. "The last text said he's coming inside."

His mind raced. This was it. Chris was going to find him. He wouldn't see how helpful Eddie was trying to be. He'd be furious. He'd call the social workers, and they'd take Eddie back. They couldn't send him back to Mom, so he didn't know where he'd go.

"Hey, look at me." Cam was crouched down in front of him. Her breath was warm on his face. "Inhale. Exhale. I don't know why you're freaking out. You're worried about Chris not thinking you're helpful. Well, look at these texts." She took his phone. "*'Please come home.' 'Come outside and we'll talk.' 'I'm coming in with you.'* Your dad isn't angry. He's worried about you."

Eddie inhaled. That made sense. *If* Cam was right about not needing to be helpful.

"Maybe we should head back to the lobby. You send a text while we still have service. Once it gets through, he'll know where to find you."

It sounded like a nice idea. Except what if Cam was wrong? Maybe Chris was just hiding his anger. Now he'd seen how unhelpful Eddie could be, and he'd changed his mind about being a family.

Eddie laughed. That was stupid.

It was scary to imagine, but it didn't make sense. Cam was right about Chris's text messages—they sounded worried. Mom had never texted him when he explored the woods all day. Chris worried about him, which meant he was thinking about him and it had nothing to do with whether Eddie had done enough chores.

Probably. Could he risk leaving without the treasure?

The chance that Chris would get tired of him was low, but the consequence of that chance was too much.

"Not yet," Eddie said. "Let's not leave yet."

"I'm telling you," Cam said, "he's more worried than mad. I wish my mom would care where I was right now."

"I believe you," Eddie said, and he was mostly telling the truth. "Dad won't get rid of me."

"Get rid of you? The hell are you talking about? He just adopted you, didn't he? I thought you were afraid of going on punishment. This 'not helpful' bullshit has you worried you'll be out on the street?"

Eddie didn't know how to respond.

"I keep saying, people yell and fight. You try to be nice—or be helpful—but sometimes you screw up. My mom tanned my hide more times than I can count, but I never worried about being thrown out. What the hell is wrong with your old mom? Come on, you text your dad, and then we're going back downstairs."

"No."

"I wasn't asking."

"If you're right, my dad still needs to save his house."

"Oh. Yeah. Well, text him that as soon as we find an elevator, we're going to the top floor."

Eddie sent a text apologizing, and telling Dad he was going to search the top floor before going back outside. It sent, but the message didn't get marked "delivered."

"I hope he sees it soon."

"Tell him what time it is for you."

Eddie sent another text.

"Okay, let's find a way up."

They walked out of the empty room, through the hole.

Twenty feet into the trashed office, a small green circle glowed near the ceiling.

"Was that there before?" Cam asked.

Eddie shook his head.

They crept towards it.

As they drew near, their flashlights revealed a single elevator. The glowing green circle had an up arrow.

"Weird," Cam said.

It's for me.

That weird thought again.

This time, it wormed its way into his head. An unwelcome intruder. He wanted a bath and some mouthwash.

This building wasn't empty or full, it was exactly what it was meant to be, and even though Eddie had no idea what that meant, it made him achy like when he had a fever.

Cam said that people should like each other whether or not they have problems. Well, this building didn't seem to want him when he was scared about Chris. Now that Cam had convinced him that maybe—just maybe—Chris would love him whether or not he was helpful, the building wormed this thought into his head that it was *for* him.

Eddie took a deep breath. None of that made any sense. It was creepy because the lights were off. Sure, it went up overnight, but scientists were always improving technology. The elevator didn't magically show up—they just hadn't noticed it before. Maybe the green light had just turned on.

"You lost in thought again?" Cam asked.

"No, I'm fine. Let's go find the treasure."

They entered the elevator and pushed the highest number: 120.

49

CHRIS SCOOTED AWAY from the open elevator shaft.

The car overlapped the door by six inches. Micah pressed her cheek to the floor, looking outside. Behind her, Roberts dropped down into the car. He must have jammed the mechanisms above.

"What's out there?" he called.

Chris looked at the wall of windows in front of him. Twenty feet across a tile floor, he was finally looking at the real edge of the skyscraper. The glass he'd seen from the outside.

Gray clouds hung low in the sky, close enough that the tower probably pierced them near its top.

He was on floor 88. From the ground, the tower had looked to be no more than 60 floors. But as Chris approached the windows and looked down, he saw the Northside of Richmond, Victorian revival homes and blocky apartments. To the south, he looked down at the modest skyscrapers of downtown.

But Chris wasn't sure what he was seeing beyond the city

itself, where there should be forests and the James River and suburbia.

Gray, instead of green. Not a light gray like the clouds, but a slate-colored jagged blur. Shadows suggested irregular, squat structures, but when he tried to focus on a single point, the landscape swirled like the first mental room they'd seen in the tower, but without color.

Down in the Northside neighborhood surrounding the tower, life continued as normal. Cars arrived and departed. People who looked small as a dime walked from cars to homes.

Chris felt a small measure of relief. The farther strangeness wasn't an apocalypse that he'd missed while inside. He was seeing something else. Maybe the spaces where Leon and Dr. Terry were trapped.

Behind him, Roberts and Micah argued. The elevator car groaned.

Chris ignored them.

He wanted to collapse into the couch at home and bury his face in the cushions. He couldn't deal with overlapping dimensions. He couldn't even deal with one dimension and living up to his responsibilities with Eddie.

Something moved behind the Richmond skyline, big, barely hidden. Organic motion blocked out the gray landscape between the bank towers and the government office buildings. When the massive thing should have come into view east of the city, it was gone.

Chris backed away from the windows. He was a mouse stalked by a lion.

Behind him, creaking and jolting from the elevator shaft.

Roberts lay on his back, hands on the upper frame of the

elevator door. With an upside-down pushup, he forced the car down with a shaking grunt.

He slid out and hopped down, chest heaving from the effort. He helped Micah down.

Micah walked to the window, eyes glued to the horizon.

"What are we looking at?" Roberts stood next to Chris.

Chris shrugged. "More reasons to find Eddie and get downstairs."

And now that he was in the outermost hall, he should be able to find that path down.

Micah breathed in, slow and loud. "The Deviser is out there."

"The what?" Chris asked.

"The builder," said Roberts. "That's what her family has always called it."

The outer room was a single corridor that wrapped around the outside of the building. The ceiling was twelve feet high. The inner wall was cinderblocks painted white. The elevator doors were the only feature on the wall.

Chris walked to the southwest corner of the building.

Roberts said something to Micah—who still stared outside—then followed behind Chris.

Out the window to the west, instead of the neighborhoods of Glen Allen, Chris saw the slate-colored unevenness that the skyline had blocked to the south. Even with a direct line of sight, his eyes refused to focus. Jagged structures rose from the hazy ground, half the height of Richmond's downtown but four times as wide. Though the periphery of his vision was clear, a blurriness sprang up whenever he tried to focus. He touched the window, wondering if it was the building shielding his view. The glass was chilly against his fingertips.

The view outside demanded his attention without revealing detail. He tried from different angles through the glass, but it didn't help. No matter how he looked at it, the Northside neighborhood directly below was the only part of his surroundings that looked normal. The farther from the building he looked, the more it hazily shifted to the dark, shifting landscape.

As if the curve of the earth had flattened out, the view went on forever.

Chris looked at his feet then squeezed his eyes shut.

His heart thumped. His missing finger throbbed. Cuts on his thigh and ear pulsed blood.

He couldn't face an infinite plane. He didn't have to. But he did want to make out the closest squat structure to the southwest. If it had been normal Richmond, the structure would have sat near the baseball diamond, home of the Flying Squirrels. A localized fog gathered around the low building that had too many angles and corners to be a baseball stadium. Chris thought if he held perfectly still, he might spot the thing quivering. He held his breath.

The tight fog bank thickened.

There was something *eternal* about the shape it contained.

The foreignness of the thought snapped Chris back to himself. He stumbled back from the glass. Blood dripped down his neck and leg. How had he let it make such a mess? He applied pressure to help it clot.

"You're pretty cut up there." Roberts came up behind him.

Chris stared purposefully at the tile floor. He couldn't

look outside again. The landscape had the hypnotic effect of the inner rooms but with less intent. He didn't feel any change in his mental state, like when the inner rooms had instilled contentment. Instead, the landscape only hypnotized.

Chris pictured Eddie's face. He thought of his boy's dimples and the way he squinted when his giggles exploded into belly laughs. He practiced his next conversation with Eddie, explaining that Sherri leaving didn't mean anyone else would leave. This morning, his goal for the day had been to make sure Eddie still felt secure, and the insanity of this tower hadn't changed that.

"You alright?" Roberts asked.

Chris stood up, his back to the windows. "No. Have you looked out there?"

Roberts shook his head. "Just enough to know that it's not for me to see."

"I should have done that from the start." Chris rubbed his temples. The fog that shifted in response to his focus and the massive thing moving behind the skyline had been disturbing enough. But the way the landscape extended infinitely—Chris didn't want to ever think about that again.

He made himself plan out his next steps.

He'd made it to the outermost edge of the building—outside where the builders had meant him to go. Or where Micah's "Deviser" had meant for him to go. This was a hidden pathway that Leon had talked about. There had to be a way back down.

He turned another corner. The building was back to its normal size out here. No extended, curved hallways. But the only doors on the inside wall were one elevator door on each side. None of them responded when he pressed the buttons.

Two air vents were on the wall in each hallway, at knee height.

He and Roberts passed Micah. Her hair hung loosely around her face. Her arms hung loosely at her sides, and her fingers twitched. Her lips moved as if she was whispering.

Roberts stopped to talk to her.

Chris crouched over an air vent.

The metal cover was the same style that Leon had inspected downstairs in the lobby. The screw heads had the same odd pattern of slits. He grabbed at them with his fingernails, but they were too tight to budge. He pushed the vent cover itself. It bent inwards.

Behind him, Roberts' voice grew more pleading.

Chris thought he could probably bust through the vent.

But not without attracting the lurchers.

Maybe one of the elevator shafts had a service ladder he could climb down.

He circled the building again, only catching glimpses of the foreign landscape outside. He pried open the other three doors. None had an easy way down.

When he made it back around, Micah faced away from the window. She stared up at Roberts, who had his hands on her shoulders. He whispered to her.

Her expression was as blank as before.

"What's she doing?" Chris asked. "Is she going to be a problem?"

A flash of light outside. He looked before he could stop himself.

Micah turned back to look outside.

Lightning flashed again, far in the distance.

This foreign landscape wasn't so foreign as to not have lightning. Maybe it wasn't as strange as Chris first thought. Maybe it had been nearby his entire life, just out of sight.

He walked back to the window, ready to jump away if he felt that hypnotic effect again.

Roberts watched the lightning over Micah's head. He blinked slowly then looked at his feet. "Let's go back to the elevator."

Chris's phone dinged.

He finally had cell service. He reached into his pocket, nicked his bandage over his little finger, and pulled out his phone. The darkening handkerchief turned bright red again.

Chris fumbled to put pressure on his hand while also reading his phone.

The time surprised him first. It was later than he'd realized, already mid-afternoon.

A text message appeared. The received time said right now, but only because that's when he received it. He couldn't know what time it was sent.

It was from Eddie.

I think the treasure is on the top floor. I'll come outside after I check.

Chris's knees went weak.

He heard Roberts warn Micah about something, but he didn't listen. He turned his back to the foreign landscape outside.

Eddie was going to the top floor.

The building wanted them at the top. Why, Chris didn't know. Maybe that's where it took people after it had finished rearranging their brains to its liking.

And now his little boy was heading up there.

Chris couldn't intercept Eddie on the way up—he had no idea where his son was, or even how long ago he'd sent that text. And the building didn't exactly let him move freely through it.

It had been corralling them upwards.

Chris couldn't stop Eddie from going to the top floor, but he could go bring him back. The elevators out here wouldn't work, so he'd need to find a way back to the inner hallways.

He thought of Leon. He'd force his way into the vents.

Micah's screams interrupted him.

50

———

CHRIS BACKED AWAY FROM MICAH.

She howled at the windows.

Roberts leaned over his boss, his thick hands on her shoulders. He whispered to her, but his wide eyes made him look the most scared Chris had seen him.

Beyond them, the flat, infinite plane drilled its way into Chris's eyes.

Micah pushed away from Roberts to pound her slender fists on the window. "Look at me!"

The ground shifted outside. Mist swirled in a moving trail. Chris thought he saw one of the short structures expand upwards.

"Micah," Roberts spoke calmly. "There's nothing out here. We should go."

She screamed again, wordless fury. She'd been spoiled by her own ability, her own determination, her own success. Micah Rayner couldn't handle failure. "Look at me!"

"We're looking," said Roberts.

"I don't think she's talking to us," Chris said.

The trail of disturbed fog banked a wide turn to point itself at the building.

"Can you hear me?" Micah yelled. "I've kept my part of the bargain. I've waited and watched and studied. And now I'm here. Give me what's mine!"

The fog expanded. Within, Chris saw flashes of gray flesh that somehow roiled like the mist hiding it. He backed away. "You coming?" he asked Roberts.

"I'm not leaving Micah to this." He clapped a hand over her mouth.

She bit him, but he lifted her off her feet.

Chris had seen enough. He couldn't force Roberts to save himself.

He ran for the vent.

Behind him, Micah freed her mouth to shout, "Do you want more? Take these two? I'll bring you whoever you want!"

Chris tried to turn the vent screws with his fingernails. If he still had his bag, he could use pliers to grab the irregular screw heads. But all he had were the clothes on his back, the rag around his hand, a busted flashlight.

The flashlight had some heft to it, though.

Micah squealed in triumph.

The room darkened behind him. Something was blocking the light from outside.

Chris forced himself not to turn around. He backed up from the vent cover.

He held the flashlight over his shoulder like a baseball bat. He charged forward, willing his momentum into the flashlight as he swung it into the vent cover. The impact jolted his wounded hand. Pain shot up his wrist.

The thin metal dented inward. It broke in three places.

He heard a shuffling down the hallway in the off-beat pattern of the lurchers' steps.

Roberts yelled a curse, and then Chris heard his heavy footsteps, fleeing in the other direction.

Chris jumped back for momentum, and again leapt forward to smash the cover with his flashlight.

The dent grew. Another two pieces of the cover snapped.

The sporadic shuffling drew closer and now came from both directions. Chris didn't dare look over his shoulder. The otherworldly appearance of the lurchers would only slow him down.

And he knew that the lurchers weren't impeded by walls or cinderblocks. One of the pale, hopping creatures could appear in front of him, face lifted, narrow tentacles waving, ready to repair the damage and prevent the perpetrator from causing anymore damage.

Chris thought of Roberts' missing fingertips after the lurcher had come for the prybar.

A chorus of deep scrapes at the windows. Micah cheered.

He kicked in the vent. His shoe went through, and then the bent metal acted like a barb to trap it.

The lurchers slid closer, loud enough now that Chris could sense them less than ten feet away.

Chris yanked his foot out. Broken metal shredded his shoe and his skin.

He dropped to the floor and threw himself through the small hole in the vent cover.

Metal dug into his shoulders. The last dregs of daylight disappeared as his hips blocked the opening of the duct. He clawed his toes for purchase and threw himself deeper into the duct.

Tentacles grazed his ankle as he jerked his foot through the hole.

He was inside.

The duct gave him two inches of clearance between his shoulders and the metal walls.

He rolled onto his back and lifted his head to look back outside.

A solid vent cover separated him from the outer corridor. Gray light painted a grid across his legs.

The lurchers had already done their repair and left.

But on the other side of the vent cover, glass cracked. Between the thin slats, he saw Micah throw her arms up in glee.

He didn't know what was outside. He hoped he'd never find out. Whatever was upstairs couldn't be as bad as what Micah had called up.

He rolled back onto his stomach. Ahead, the duct extended into darkness. Chris gripped his broken flashlight tightly.

Chris crawled forward, away from the chaos behind him.

51

———

CHRIS SCRAMBLED THROUGH ABSOLUTE DARKNESS. With his wounded hand, he tapped the flashlight against the bottom of the duct in front of him.

The metal on metal echoed ahead.

At the first intersection Chris found, he turned left towards the center of the building.

His panic at Eddie going to the top floor was more contained now that Chris had a plan. His gut said the top floor was bad news, but this whole building was bad news. At least now he knew where Eddie was and could go get him.

Gravity yanked the flashlight out of his hand.

It clanged against the duct walls as it fell, then slammed into another floor after less than two seconds.

He'd found a path down.

Right when he needed to go up.

Still, it would be good to test whether this was actually a way down, to use after he found Eddie.

Chris lowered himself down the ductwork.

He pressed against either side of the vertical duct, shimmying in quick bursts until he found the bottom. He'd gone down two floors at most. Still eighty-five to get to the bottom, but now he knew there was a way down.

Now to find a way up to the top.

He hurried through the ducts, always turning closer to the interior of the building. He found another drop but crawled across it this time.

Another sharp right-angled turn, and he saw a grid of fluorescent lights. A vent cover to an inner hallway.

He kicked it out, then hurried through it as the lurchers arrived.

He backed up to let the freakish things make their repairs. The flickering white light overhead lit up only a small patch of the curved hallway. The air was chillier in here—it numbed the open wound where his finger used to be.

Chris looked around. The lights on this floor were few and far between. The next one was at least two hundred feet away. Chris thought he saw movement in the dark stretches between.

But past the next fluorescent light was the soft glow of an elevator lobby.

Chris ran towards it. He felt like a little boy running from the bathroom to his bedroom at night, refusing to look to either side for risk of coming face-to-face with the boogey-man. Or in Chris's case now, seeing the cinderblock walls turn organic, then reach out to swallow him.

He ran under the next light fixture, then reached the lobby.

The walls spun. He leaned on the elevator door. How much blood had he lost?

He looked up at the LED screen above the doors.

Focusing took effort, but he could do it. He was on floor eighty-four.

He pushed the up buttons on both elevators. No response.

His heartbeat thumped in his hand.

Another push of the button, still no response.

Chris pounded on the door. "First you try to force us up there, and now you won't let me?"

The building didn't want him to get to Eddie.

Except that didn't feel quite right. The building was a building. It may have been built with a purpose, but it couldn't change its mind about specific people.

Chris inhaled slowly. He couldn't reason his way into the doors opening.

He felt a familiar tug in his mind. A major setback. He could jump from setback to setback, failure to failure. That's what he did with his job search—circling around his own failure. He'd failed here, too. Failed to stop Eddie from entering the building. Failed to find him.

Chris mentally swatted away that incursive train of thought.

He couldn't make those same mistakes as before. Eddie needed him.

There were other elevators to try on this floor. And if they didn't open, he'd go back into the ductwork to work his way up, one floor at a time.

It occurred to him that this mindset would have been helpful in dealing with failure after rejected job applications. Even in dealing with Sherri leaving.

He could think about that later. Now he had to find a way up to Eddie.

The elevator doors slid open.

He hesitated. It could be a trap.

Of course it was a trap. But Eddie was the bait, and that meant Chris had no choice but to spring it.

He walked through the doors, trying to figure out how he had reasoned the elevator into opening.

The button for the 120th floor was already lit.

The doors closed, and Chris rose skyward to find his son.

52

THE DOORS OPENED to reveal floor 120.

Orange fog hung low over what looked like a commercial office space after a riot. A central light source somewhere ahead reflected in the mist like a car's high beams, shrinking visibility.

Chris could see no more than twenty feet. Toppled cubicle walls were piled atop each other, forming a hill that disappeared upwards into the mist. A pile of copy machines was stacked just as haphazardly. The machines on the floor sank into the tile, joined like Chris's finger had with Leon's.

Chris stepped forward into the valley between the mountains of office equipment.

Tile shifted beneath his feet. The floor was made up of stacks of square tiles. Chris peered into the cracks. The light reached three feet down, but the unstable stacks of tile went even deeper.

His gut said to flee. Every creeping bit of insanity in the building below had dripped down from the madness that was the top floor.

The orange mist was too similar to the mist around Dr. Terry when he'd pleaded for help. And it was too close to the mist outside that hid the roiling flesh of the thing that came to see Micah.

Anything could be hiding up here, lurking behind piles of office equipment, hiding in the otherworldly fog.

Eddie was up here.

Chris expected that once Eddie stepped out of the elevators, seeking treasure, he'd have taken one look around and then tried to leave.

Chris looked behind him at the two elevator doors. The elevator bank was a little hut disconnected from the outer walls. Not that Chris could see the outer walls in any direction.

He tried the down buttons. Nothing.

"Eddie?" he called.

Once Eddie realized the elevator wouldn't take him back down, he'd have looked for stairs. But there weren't any nearby doors. When Eddie didn't immediately spot stairs, where would he have gone? Any other kid would have sat and waited. But Eddie tried to fix things. He would have thought up a plan—no smarter than any other nine-year-old's—and then instantly put it into action.

Chris looked around. The thick mist hid everything except the phased-together copy machines and the mound of cubicle walls.

And the bright glow, somewhere deep within the orange fog. The only option for a little boy desperate for a plan.

Chris followed the light.

Past the valley of cubicles and copiers, Chris found a forest of black poles. He rapped his knuckles on one. They were pulldown screens for projectors, stuck down inside the stacks of tile. Black liquid pooled in the cracks and crevices.

Chris passed through the forest, moving toward the light. Ink stained his shoes.

He stumbled and almost fell into an open hole. He grabbed a projector screen and held tight. His wounded hand started bleeding again.

The pit was ten feet across and went twenty feet down before it curved. Its edges were lined with desks and office chairs. Orange fog sank around the curve and out of sight. It reminded Chris of a bathtub drain.

Cursing to himself, he circled the maw. This wasn't what he'd expected. What about this office junkyard would help mental health? After everything else, Chris wouldn't have been surprised to see a fully functioning counseling center on the top floor.

But there was no calming feeling. Despite the junkyard of office furniture, it felt *empty*. Unfinished. This was where the builders had discarded their extra materials, not dumping them like a normal landfill but placing them in space following the same logic and methods they'd used to instantly construct this tower.

Chris started to walk away from the pit, and then a terrible thought occurred to him.

He turned on his phone's flashlight to look deeper into the hole. The LED white light reflected off chair legs and steel desktops.

"Eddie?" he called down.

If the path to the light passed directly over this pit, Eddie could have fallen in.

But Eddie was nimbler than Chris. He could swing across

monkey bars like their namesake. Born to wealthier parents, he might have been a gymnast. He wouldn't have fallen here.

Chris called his name again, this time turning around, towards the light.

No response.

Metal scraped on metal somewhere off to his right. He peered into the orange fog.

The tiles were piled higher in that direction, forming an irregular staircase.

He bounced on his heels, ready to flee if Leon or Dr. Terry came staggering down out of the mist.

Chris waited for the scraping sound to repeat itself. Nothing. He continued toward the light.

He called for Eddie again.

A hand closed around his mouth. He was yanked backwards, against a warm body.

Roberts whispered into his ear, "Keep quiet. Micah's hunting."

53

———

EDDIE HELD tight to Cam's hand.

He did not like this top floor.

The dark rooms downstairs were better than the fog up here. It looked like someone spilled orange Kool-Aid into a smoke machine.

Eddie thought it was neat when the door first opened and he saw those piles of copy machines and cubicle walls. It'd be fun to climb a playground like that.

But then he noticed the way the edges of the copy machines were stuck into the tile floor. Like they'd been halfway sucked in.

"Let's look for the treasure somewhere else," Eddie had suggested. He didn't want to walk between the two creepy piles of work stuff, so they'd circled the little hut with the elevators.

"Same shit back here." Cam squeezed Eddie's hand and smiled down at him. But she looked as worried as he felt.

This place wasn't right. Behind the elevator hut, the mist drifted through a huge tangle of cables. They were black and beige and orange, and the whole jumble could have hidden ten school buses. It made Eddie think of the wall of brambles in *Sleeping Beauty*.

"Let's go around," Cam said.

Eddie agreed.

"What do you think we're looking for?" Cam led him by the hand over cracked tile. She kept the cables out of reach to their right, which made Eddie happy since he kept picturing an orange rubber cord snaking out to wrap around his ankle.

"Something worth a lot of money. That man wouldn't have hired my dad otherwise." He kept his eyes straight ahead. The orange mist didn't let him see far.

"Yeah, but what? When you knew specific spots to look, we didn't have to know what we were looking for exactly. Now that we're looking all over, we gotta have an idea of what it looks like. How else are we gonna spot it?"

She had a point. But Eddie didn't know what the treasure was, only that the man in the driveway wanted to pay dad a lot of money to find it.

"That dude who hired your dad, what'd he look like? What was he wearing?"

Eddie closed his eyes to remember. "A fuzzy coat. Big glasses. He looked smart."

"Did he look like a gangster? Like from the movies? Maybe it's a suitcase full of money. Or some stolen diamonds."

Eddie didn't know how they'd ever find diamonds in this mess, even if they were as big as the diamond in those D.C. museums.

"He looked like a librarian," Eddie decided.

"Maybe it's some rare books."

They approached something blurry ahead. As they walked closer, it grew more clear.

"What the hell is this?" Cam whispered.

Big pipes stuck up out of the floor, stopping at shoulder-height. Big enough around for Eddie to fit inside, not that he would.

"Could be treasure inside one of them." Cam let go of Eddie's hand to go peek down through the open top of the nearest.

Eddie hurried behind her.

Cam leaned over, and light from within the pipe lit her face in a shifting gray glow. Her eyes went wide.

"What is it?" Eddie leaned forward, but Cam held him back.

"Let me see!"

"It goes all the way down," Cam said stiffly. "We only saw that one guy, right? There's so many people in here."

"Do you see my Dad?" Eddie tried to push forward again.

"They're all working. Something's making them work. I think they're dead, but they can't stop."

Eddie didn't like the way that Cam leaned closer to the pipe's opening. Her nose almost went inside. "Let's go back," he pleaded.

"We should help them, right? We can't leave them. They'll never finish working. They gotta leave." She got more freaked out. "Don't they know they gotta leave? Oh god, what if they can't?"

Eddie grabbed the back of Cam's belt and pulled. She resisted.

"We can help them. Grab some of those plugs."

Eddie wasn't going anywhere near the cable-bramble

bush. This wasn't a treasure hunt anymore. This wasn't just a dark, weird office building. He'd marched into a scary movie, and he wanted to go home. "Please, let's go. I'm scared."

"Maybe you should look. You'll see what I mean."

Whatever was in there, it had hypnotized her. Eddie punched Cam's thigh as hard as he could.

She ignored him. "Here comes one! Hey! Let me help you."

A dirty arm reached up out of the pipe. Orange dust caked on the fingers. Splits in the skin revealed dusty blood.

Cam screamed. The hand grabbed her hair.

No—it stuck in her hair. Her brown braids went in the palm and out the back of the hand.

"Oh fuck!" Cam tried to pull away.

A shoulder appeared, then the top of a head. Moaning, begging from in the pipe.

Eddie couldn't run away. He had to be helpful.

Cam fell. The arm reached down over the edge of the pipe.

Eddie grabbed a broken piece of floor tile.

Cam screamed. The man crawling out of the pipe yelled in Spanish. He wore an old shirt that looked like it was from a cowboy movie.

Cam tried to crawl backwards, but her hair tugged the man's hand along with her. Cuts and orange dust covered his face. He squinted, and Eddie realized he could barely see them.

Eddie pushed the sharpest edge of the tile against Cam's hair to pin the braid against the metal pipe. He worked it back and forth.

The man stared through Eddie, then swiped his free hand

at Eddie's face. Eddie ducked. The man sobbed Spanish words that Eddie didn't know.

He saw the texture of the metal pipe through the man's body. He was like smoke. That made Eddie's stomach flop, so he closed his eyes and pushed harder on the tile.

His hand suddenly hurt and felt wet.

Cam scrambled away.

Eddie opened his eyes.

The clear man was gone.

Cam hugged him around the waist to pull him away. "Forget your treasure. We're leaving."

They ran back through the mist, staying far away from the cable-bramble bush. Eddie refused to look back over his shoulder at the pipes.

It felt like an eternity, but the elevator hut finally appeared.

Cam mashed the button. The doors opened.

They rushed inside and pushed the button for the bottom floor.

Nothing happened. The doors didn't close. The LED screen didn't change from 120. Nothing *dinged*.

"Why won't it let us go down?" Cam sounded terrified.

Eddie didn't know how to handle a teenager being scared. "I'll try again," he said. He ran out of the elevator to push the down button again.

The doors closed.

"No!" he yelled.

Cam called his name, and her voice descended.

Eddie slammed his hand against the doors. He pushed the buttons over and over.

"Please," he begged no one.

He didn't want to turn around. The weird piles of office furniture were behind him. And there were probably more pipes on the other side.

But he couldn't wait for an elevator that didn't want him.

Somewhere, there had to be stairs. He'd find them.

"Hello, little buddy."

Eddie spun around. His heart pounded from the shock. It didn't slow down when he saw the skinny old woman. She looked like a skeleton wrapped in tight skin. Her reddish-gray hair was frazzly. The tips of her boney fingers dripped blood.

"Your daddy was looking for you." She reached out and blood splattered on Eddie's cheeks.

Eddie ran.

54

———

CHRIS TRIED TO TURN AROUND, but Roberts held him still.

"How'd you get up here?" Chris hissed. He wobbled on the tiered hill of tiles. It descended like a haphazard staircase, into the orange fog, toward the bright light.

Roberts shushed him. When he determined it was quiet enough, he whispered, "I jumped across the elevator shaft, back to the inner hallways. Then the elevator took me the rest of the way up."

"Why didn't you just leave?"

"I had to see. That thing out there couldn't have been the Deviser. I came up here to find the real Deviser."

"Did you find it?"

Roberts shook his head. He motioned to the fog and office detritus. "Does this feel like the work of a benevolent entity to you?"

Tile clattered together, back the way they'd come from.

Micah's voice called out through the fog. It was raspier than before. "I hear you. You'll give me what's mine!"

Something heavy and metallic struck the tile. Shattered bits of it scattered and bounced towards them.

Micah was bringing the lurchers.

Chris crept down the hill of tiles. Roberts followed, then stopped him again. His eyes darted over Chris's head, tracking something. He touched his finger to his lips.

Orange mist curled around him. Ahead, the stacks of tiles shortened, forming a downward slope that led to a sunken plot with a grid of toilets, sinks, and broken mirrors.

"How'd Micah get up here?" Chris asked.

"Something must have helped her. When that thing approached her, I ran and was on an elevator within thirty seconds. But she was waiting for me at the top."

It was one more impossible thing on top of all the rest, but Micah's quick journey threatened him more directly than the rest. More than ever, he wanted to find Eddie and escape. "You said she was hunting. What's she hunting?"

"Us," Roberts whispered.

"You could break her in half. What are you scared of?"

"Anyone can summon the lurchers." He rubbed the nubs of his fingers.

"Why would she want that?" Chris tried not to think of Eddie lost in this mess, encountering a pale, dizzying lurcher. "My son's in here. I need to find him."

Roberts motioned for Chris to follow. They rounded the sunken plot of bathroom fixtures to enter a forest of duct-work. Dull silver boxes emerged from the floor and then branched into a chaotic canopy above their heads.

They squatted in a nook next to an aluminum y-junction.

Roberts' gaze darted from shadow to shadow. "Why do you think your boy's in here?"

Chris explained the text messages.

Roberts listened intently. "We need to find him before Micah. That thing—not the Deviser—did something to her mind."

Chris suspected it had only amplified the tyrannical obsession already in Micah's mind. She'd dominated her industry by walking on people—why stop now?

"She's trying to offer me up to the counterfeit Deviser," said Roberts. "You too, now. She'll probably do the same to him."

"But the lurchers repair the building. How does getting them to hurt us help her?"

"Either there's something we don't understand about them, or her mind is just damaged."

"Okay, then we need to find Eddie before she does. He would have headed toward the light."

"Micah was hovering around there before you showed up and started shouting."

"Then let's get there quick."

Roberts squeezed his eyes shut, breathed deep, then nodded. "Alright, but you need to understand something. Micah and I were wrong about this building. Whatever's been helping mankind with the other buildings, that's something else. If the Deviser is an angel, this counterfeit is a demon. I should have realized it as soon as we saw the crazy mental floors. This building is nothing like the others."

"You're wasting time."

"I need you to understand that I never meant for anyone to get hurt. This building is a counterfeit."

That didn't ring true to Chris. This building wasn't like the others, but it did feel like the next step in the progression.

The others brought people close together. And now that people were living tightly in cities, this one would... Chris wasn't sure. It healed mental issues. But it had also swallowed Leon and Dr. Terry.

"When we first built feeding troughs for wild animals, we must have seemed like angels." Chris walked through the ductwork forest toward the orange light.

Roberts followed. "What are you talking about?"

"Then when we built warm barns for them to sleep in. They were comfortable. But they were also nearby for our easy access."

Chris reached the edge of the ductwork forest. The mist was thicker—he could feel moisture on his skin.

Past the forest, a cracked plane of stacked floor tiles. Through the thick orange fog, the central light grew brighter.

"This isn't a slaughterhouse," Roberts said. "We're not cattle. The Deviser—the true Deviser—has been helping mankind for millennia."

"It's funneled us into cities. And now we've been funneled to the top floor. What's at the end of the chute? Cattle get a quick death from a pneumatic gun." Chris pointed to the light through the fog. "What do we get?"

Roberts whispered, "No."

"What did Leon and Dr. Terry get? What did your Deviser do to Micah?"

"That's not the Deviser," Roberts growled.

"You saw the same flat dimension outside as I did. Was there anything out there that felt benevolent?"

"This demon imposter could be from another plane of reality."

"Answer my question." Chris needed Roberts to accept

what was happening if they were going to escape. "This building fits the pattern you and Micah were searching for. But has anything here felt like it was designed to help people?"

Roberts hugged his arms across his chest. "It's not the Deviser. The Deviser loves us. I could feel that thing's hate. Micah watched it and whispered to herself. She doesn't care whether it's the real Deviser, as long as it gives her what she's been searching for: the next breakthrough that'll make her even more rich and powerful."

And now, Eddie was up here with her. This conversation was wasting time.

Chris stepped out of the ductwork forest onto the cracked tile plane. These stacks were several inches from each other, and each step sent individual tiles sliding around. It was like walking on ice.

Roberts followed behind. Tile cracked under his weight.

From far ahead through the mist, a child yelled, surprise wrapped up in anger.

Chris ran to find his son.

55

———

CHRIS SCRAMBLED over the stacks of tile. Orange fog blew past his cheeks.

The light through the mist grew brighter.

"Eddie!" he called.

The only response was the tile clinking against itself as Roberts lumbered behind him.

"What's the plan?" Roberts asked.

Chris's footing wobbled, then he continued on. "Find Eddie. Find a way back down."

"I meant with Micah. If we get close, she'll bring the lurchers after us."

"If she's a threat to my son, I'll deal with her." Chris heard the hubris in his voice, threatening this bodyguard's client and friend.

But Roberts didn't object.

The light grew brighter to the point that Chris had to squint through the orange fog. Under his feet, the gaps between stacks of tile grew wider. Every wobbling step he took sent a low tower toppling.

He called for his son again.

From ahead, off to the side of the brightness, a response. "Dad?"

A mixture of relief and terror filled Chris. Eddie was still okay; Eddie was stuck in this tower with him. And with Micah.

"Come to my voice," Chris yelled.

Eddie's footsteps, hopping from stack of tile to stack of tile, sounded through the fog.

Chris ran towards them.

Eddie appeared out of the mist. A smeared shape at first, barely visible through the light reflecting on the moisture in the air. Then more defined as Chris saw Eddie's Spiderman t-shirt, grass-stained blue jeans, and the red Nikes that Chris had bought him last week. Finally Chris saw Eddie's face. Shaggy hair, tousled from anxious pulling. Lips tight with repressed fear. Green eyes pleaded with Chris to make this nightmare end.

Chris braced himself on a steady stack of tile and lifted his son.

Eddie was nearly ten and weighed a solid hundred pounds. Chris was exhausted, and his wounded hand throbbed. But he found the strength to hold his son.

"I couldn't find the treasure." Eddie buried his face in Chris's shoulder. "I tried to be helpful. I'm sorry."

Chris cooed, "It's okay. I'm not mad. Are you okay? You're not hurt?"

"An invisible man tried to hurt my friend, but we got away."

He'd thought he knew terror before, but the idea of Leon or Dr. Terry going after Eddie rocked Chris to his core. "I won't let anyone get you."

Roberts patted Eddie's back. "You have a friend up here?"

Eddie flinched away from the giant man. But he saw Roberts' earnest smile and relaxed. "My friend went back down the elevator. She didn't mean to leave me alone."

"You're okay. You're not alone now," Chris promised.

Roberts crouched, still taller than Eddie by a foot. "You're either brave or stupid, going on a treasure hunt like this."

"Brave," Eddie said.

"He's got reckless momentum." Chris felt pride for his determined son. "He'll own a booming business one day if I can keep him alive long enough." His own joke felt sick considering their present circumstances. "Eddie, why did you think there was treasure in here?"

Eddie wriggled his way out of Chris's embrace. "The man in the driveway wanted to hire you to find it."

"You misunderstood. But he's a jerk anyways." Chris knew he shouldn't speak ill of the dead, but he wasn't positive Dr. Terry was dead, and if anyone deserved ill words, it was the old man who'd got them into this situation to start with.

"I'm sorry I wasn't helpful enough and Mom left."

"What?"

"I tried to do enough chores."

Roberts gave Chris an awkward look as if to say, *better deal with this.*

"Mom left because she wanted a new life," Chris said.

"With kids more helpful than me."

"I don't think she wants *any* kids." That was stupid. That's not what Eddie needed to hear. "Wait, that's not what I meant. I mean, she left because she didn't want to be married to me anymore. It has nothing to do with you."

Anger flared inside Chris, and then his body went weak. He'd sleep alone tonight. Make breakfast alone tomorrow.

No, tomorrow was Saturday. On Saturdays, Eddie helped him make pancakes.

He took a breath. He shouldn't be feeling heartbreak while on the top floor of a deadly, impossible skyscraper.

"But I wasn't helpful enough," Eddie said. "That's why I had to leave my old mom."

"No. Somebody told you wrong. Your old mom tried her best, but she failed. You came to us so you could be happier."

Eddie scrunched his eyebrows. "Mom didn't give me a hug goodbye."

Chris didn't know which mom he meant.

"Ah fuck," breathed Roberts.

Chris jerked his head around, looking for the threat. He expected to see Micah charging with the light at her back, wielding a taser and pepper spray. Or lurchers shambling towards them. Or Dr. Terry and Leon, sickly gray and eager to yank Eddie off to wherever they'd been taken.

But then Roberts said, "Hey now, your daddy gives good hugs, doesn't he?"

Eddie nodded.

"And he's not giving you any 'goodbye' hugs. Just good morning or good night hugs. This guy's not going anywhere."

"I know," Eddie whispered. "Can we go home now?"

"Of course." Chris looked around. The constant bright light helped him maintain his bearings—he knew which way led back to the elevators—but the fog still kept visibility short and close.

"The elevator wouldn't open back up," Eddie said. "It did for Cam, but not for me."

That was a puzzle they didn't have time for. Why did the elevator only open for some people? Better to skip the brainteaser.

"We'll find another way down. Any ideas?" Chris asked Roberts. But he feared the elevators were the only exit.

"Did you see that pit with the desks and chairs? Maybe it goes down to the next floor."

"Maybe it leads to Leon and Dr. Terry. Or to outside—the other version of outside." Chris imagined helping Eddie climb down the mishmash of chair legs, unable to know what was around the bend. "We need a stairwell. Or ducts we can climb down."

"Let's find the edge of this room," suggested Roberts. "Another outer hallway might have what we need."

Chris shook his head. "This room went beyond the elevators. Downstairs, the outer hallway was on the other side. Up here, I don't even know if there's an outer wall at all." Everything was pointing back to the elevators. He couldn't figure out the building's appetites—he just wanted a path downstairs.

Tile tapped tile somewhere out in the fog. Roberts snapped to attention. "Seems like if the building wants us, the building will take us."

Gears turned in Chris's mind. "You don't think it's random who was taken?"

"You said it yourself—this building is like a slaughter-house chute."

"I said everything the Deviser has created is like that," Chris said. "It brought us closer together in cities, and now it's driven us up this tower."

"I'll give you this tower. That's all. The Deviser Micah

taught me about is good. But you're right about this building. It drove us upwards, just like the slaughterhouse workers drive cattle towards their final stall."

"Why hasn't it taken us? Why'd it take Leon and Dr. Terry?"

Roberts shrugged. "I don't know. But if we can figure out why then maybe we can convince it to let us leave."

"We can't leave?" Eddie asked.

"Sure we can," Chris said. "We're deciding the best way out right now."

"You were with both of them before they disappeared," Roberts said. "What did they do? What did they say?"

Trying to stay outwardly calm made Chris feel his exhaustion. "I'm not sure. Leon was talking about building hacking. He was excited because he hadn't done it in a while. And Dr. Terry... he was losing his mind. He was rambling apologies for fucking up my career."

Eddie gasped and then giggled at his dad swearing. The innocent sound felt sour against their unnatural surroundings.

Roberts scratched his cheek. "And they didn't step in the wrong place, or touch the wall, or anything like that?"

Chris exhaled. "I couldn't tell you."

"You've got to. We figure out what it wants, and maybe we can get out."

Chris held tight to Eddie's hand.

It was a stupid plan. A long shot. Even if they figured something out, what could they do with that info? But the elevators wouldn't let them back down, and there was no sign of a stairwell. Even if he found the ventilation system like he'd used down below, it'd take days to crawl down one hundred-twenty floors.

This was the only plan they had.

"Alright. Let's go over what we know."

Eddie wandered towards the light. "I was going to look out the window. We could try that."

Chris and Roberts exchanged a thoughtful look. Chris had assumed the light was unnatural, but maybe it was a window, and the sun had broken through the clouds outside.

"It's worth checking out," Roberts said. "If it's a window, there's a wall, and there could be stairs. Just keep an eye out for Micah."

If it was a way down without puzzling out why and when the elevator worked, Chris was for it.

"Let's do it." Chris took Eddie's hand and led the way towards the light.

56

THEY WALKED around a pit of steel framing studs and between piles of rolled-up carpet stacked higher than they could see.

The light grew brighter.

Twice they heard someone behind them. Roberts fell back to frequently check over his shoulder. Micah was hunting them, and she'd bring the lurchers.

Chris tried to squash the hope he felt growing inside. If Eddie was right, and it was a window and sunlight, then maybe there was a way down. He expected that out the window would be the same otherworldly landscape that he'd seen out the window below. But if there was a wall, there may be a stairwell.

"See it, Dad?" Eddie tugged on Chris's hand to point at the light.

Chris squinted through the orange fog, now turned yellow with the whiteness of the light.

The fog thinned out to reveal a blindingly bright rectangle.

They'd reached a wall, like any other wall down below.

Cinderblock painted white. Close to the blinding light, the paint was dried and flaking.

No ceiling was visible, even with the thinner fog allowing Chris to see forty feet above. The cinderblock continued upwards out of sight.

The bright rectangle itself—or window, if it was a window—was ten feet wide and twice as tall. Chris couldn't tell if it was glass that faced a blinding sun or a flat surface that itself shone with blinding light. He closed his eyes and turned away.

When he opened them, he saw Eddie, slack-jawed, staring at the light. His pupils were pinpricks, his body doing what it could to protect Eddie from his own actions.

Chris stepped between his son and the light.

Eddie looked up at Chris. His shoulders hung loose. He smiled. Dimples appeared in his cheeks. "Can I see it again?"

"The light? What did you see?"

"I like it. Like when I sat between you and Mom, and we watched Spider-man."

That had been after an especially bad week at his bio mom's house, and the social worker had filed an emergency order to get Eddie removed quickly.

Chris looked over his shoulder. He squinted into the light.

His eyes tingled, and then that feeling extended into his head and down his spine. Even with the pain from his missing finger, the cuts down his back, and the aches in his muscles, he felt more comfortable. He didn't need to run away.

Scratch that—this building was wildly dangerous, and he needed to get himself and his son out of here. But the anxiety that accompanied those thoughts before was gone. His level of confidence that he could escape hadn't changed, only his body's stress reaction.

He looked back down at Eddie. The terror of raising an emotionally damaged boy by himself was gone. It would be difficult, and maybe he'd make awful mistakes. But thinking about it no longer sent his heart pounding and his palms sweating.

Roberts stood behind them, peering curiously at the light. "You felt that, didn't you?"

"I think so," Chris said.

"It's like it reached into my brain and fixed it. Look," he pointed next to the window.

Tough to see past the light's glare, pipes ran alongside the window, leading into the light on one end and down into the floor on the other.

"That's what's powering everything," Chris said. "That's the same energy that's in all the central rooms."

His curiosity got the better of him and he looked again. He couldn't tell whether the pipes were going through an open window, or attached directly to a glowing panel. Regardless, this seemed to be the source of the mental and emotional energy that he'd felt in the room with the miniature sun or the room with the neon slides. This building was designed to fix minds, and this was the power source.

The tingling entered through his eyes again, down into his body. He thought of his career, hijacked by a single man, and for the first time in four years, he didn't feel hate when he thought of him. He thought of his future career prospects. He was in a shitty spot, no portfolio, four years into his career. If he wanted to stay an architect, it wouldn't be easy. But he would make it work, or he wouldn't. It'd hurt, and he'd always doubt whether he bailed too soon, but life would go on. He thought of his house. If he and Eddie had to move, that would be tough. He'd leave the house where he and Sherri had fallen more deeply in love—and then fallen out of love. Eddie would have one more rug yanked out from under him. But he and Eddie would still be together. It was cheaper to live in the suburbs anyways. Or he could see if his parents would take them in. Chris's dad loved Eddie. Chris had no intention of moving to small-town Virginia with his parents indefinitely, but maybe it'd be a good space to regroup while he and Eddie figured things out.

Sherri was gone, and it hurt. But Chris would mourn for a while and then be okay again.

As he thought over his life, none of his problems went away. None of the worst case scenarios he imagined changed. What changed was that his mind considered those worst case scenarios only with the same likelihood as any other outcome. And his physical reaction was gone.

"Is this what people without anxiety feel like all the time?" he whispered.

"Huh?" Eddie leaned around him to look again.

"I don't know if you should," Chris said but didn't stop him.

Roberts let out a single sob.

"What is it?" Chris asked.

The big man shrugged. "I don't hate my ex-wife."

"That's... good."

"It's not just that. Look at this," he gestured at the light. "It's amazing. This could change people's lives everywhere."

"You think this is what Micah was hoping to find?"

He shook his head. "The Deviser is good. Was good. All

the other buildings brought people together. Then this one, what did it do to Dr. Terry and Leon? And that thing we saw through the window downstairs—you and me both felt how wrong it was."

"What thing?" Eddie asked.

"Nothing," Chris said.

"But now this," Roberts said. "This right here was built by the same Deviser that gave us pane glass and air conditioning and steel towers. I wanted to believe it was two separate builders, but it's not. And if the same thing that took Dr. Terry and Leon and is making them suffer, if that same thing built this, then what is this for?"

Something shattered at their feet, and they all jumped.

A glass paperweight had flown in from the orange mist and left a crack in the floor.

Another landed at their feet. The floor broke with an audible crack.

Micah shrieked triumph from somewhere in the fog.

A wall of lurchers approached them.

57

———

Chris picked up Eddie, who frantically looked around.

"Who's that? Is it the old lady?"

Micah yelled again. "I've worked too hard for this!"

The sounds of lurchers came through the fog from all directions, hopping and dragging themselves along the tile.

Chris staggered away from Micah's voice. His thighs ached. His hand throbbed, and he felt blood seep through the bandage. Eddie was too heavy, and he was exhausted.

Roberts scooped Eddie into his arms.

"Dad?" Eddie whined.

"It's okay. He can carry you faster. We're gonna run now."

They ran along the wall, away from Micah's screamed threats and the shattering of the tile floor as she smashed it.

Chris ran alongside Roberts, who spoke calmingly to Eddie as his long gait jostled the boy.

A loose brick clattered past their feet.

Shadows in the orange mist ahead revealed themselves to be a wall of lurchers, heading for Micah, with Chris, Eddie, and Roberts in their way. They hunched forward, and the gaps in their blank faces slid open to unleash the writhing swarm of tentacles.

Roberts turned so Eddie couldn't see them. "When they get close," he said, "I'll toss your boy overtop of them."

"They're not after us," Chris said. "They want to fix the floor."

Roberts waggled his wounded fingertips. "If we're in the way, they'll fix us, too."

Eddie wriggled to try to get down. "What's that mean?"

Roberts held him tight.

"Just walk forward," Chris hissed. "Slowly."

They crept away from the brick and the gouge in the floor.

Eddie craned his neck enough to see behind him. He spotted the lurchers—now less than ten feet away—and let out a fearful moan.

Roberts squeezed him to his chest. Chris reached over to hold Eddie's trembling hand.

"They don't care about us," Chris whispered. "Close your eyes and they'll leave."

The lurchers hopped and dragged themselves closer. Chris and Roberts played a delicate game of Red Rover, finding gaps in the oncoming wall of creatures.

One brushed Chris's shoulder, and pain exploded in his flesh, the same as when Leon had merged their fingers. Then the lurcher continued past, and the pain vanished.

Chris caught his breath. "Keep moving."

He watched as Eddie stared in terror at the lurchers over Roberts' shoulder, then positioned himself so his son couldn't see.

He quickly searched for anything on the cinderblock wall —doors, windows, vents—but it was blank.

Something crashed into the tile between Chris and Roberts, then bounced to a stop ahead of them. It was a disk drive, ripped out of a computer, or plucked from an abandoned pile of them somewhere on this top floor.

Another smashed down off to Chris's left.

Chris looked over his shoulder. A lurcher leapt towards him. It came down well short, and folded over to fix the damage to the floor.

More office junk crashed around their feet.

A glass paperweight struck Roberts in the head, then bounced to the floor, which it cracked. Roberts fell to his knees. His weight dented the tile. He dropped Eddie.

Chris yanked Eddie to his feet and tried to do the same for Roberts. "Get up, let's go."

Roberts squeezed his eyes shut. He grunted.

Another paperweight hit the floor to bounce into Chris's shin. Lurchers hopped towards them. Chris pulled on Roberts' wrist. "Get up."

Eddie tried to help, pulling on his other wrist.

"I can't..." Roberts got one foot under him, then fell again. His hip hit the floor. It bashed a shallow crater in the weak tile.

"Daddy!" Eddie yelled.

A lurcher appeared from the mist. It folded over, lowering its head towards Eddie. Its blank face slid open, and tentacles slithered out.

Chris shoved Eddie out of its path.

Roberts still lay atop the damage his fall had caused.

Chris dropped into a squat, braced his hands against

Roberts' side, and shoved. Roberts tried to help, seemingly still aware of the danger he was in, rolling to the side, but then his weight crashed back down.

Eddie ran to Chris's side to help push.

"No!" Chris yelled. "Get away."

Eddie pushed anyways as the lurcher dipped its tentacles into Roberts' shoulder. Roberts screamed. He flinched upwards, and in that movement, Chris and Eddie pushed him hard enough to roll him onto his back, away from the damaged floor.

Eddie's momentum carried him into the yellow leathery side of the lurcher.

Eddie screamed.

Chris felt his son's pain in every cell of his body.

Eddie fell into the lurcher, sharing the same space from his shoulders to his gut.

Chris dove for his son. He grabbed Eddie's hands to drag him away from the lurcher and into his arms.

Eddie sobbed into Chris's chest. Eddie squeezed him. "It's okay. It's over."

He knew the pain was gone, that Eddie was now only crying from the shock of it. He wanted to make it so Eddie had never felt that pain, but he couldn't change the past.

A loose door handle flew out of the mist. Chris reached up and caught it.

"I won't let her hurt you again." He picked up the glass paperweight. It was heavier than it looked. It had broken to leave a jagged edge.

He looked Eddie in the eye. "I need you to stay with Roberts until he can stand up again."

Eddie stared at the lurcher as it hovered its face inches

over the cracked floor, its tentacles quivering against the damage. "No, I'm coming with you."

"Roberts, can you keep Eddie here with you?"

Roberts grabbed Eddie's ankle. "Stay with me a couple minutes. Your dad will be right back."

Eddie kicked. "No!"

"I promise, I'm not leaving you."

Roberts locked eyes with Chris. He looked at the jagged paperweight in Chris's hand. He still looked dizzy, but a calm knowing rested in his expression. He nodded.

Chris walked into the orange fog.

58

———

CHRIS FOUND Micah twenty feet back.

She stood atop a low hill of EXIT signs which all glowed green. She'd found a shoulder bag to fill with doorknobs, paperweights, computer drives, and anything else heavy and throwable.

Chris adjusted the glass paperweight in his hand. He held it so the jagged edge pointed down.

Micah's hair was wild. The little makeup she wore smeared black around her eyes. Her forehead already had a gash in it, as well as her hand. She must have fallen.

The calm, controlled authority that she carried in her gaze had been replaced with mania.

She held a chunk of tile, arm cocked back, ready to throw.

Chris squeezed his weapon. He avoided imagining what it would feel like to strike this old woman. "You get one chance to walk away."

Micah laughed. It devolved into a giggle. "So you can follow me down?"

Chris loosened his grip. "Do you know a way out?"

"The elevators."

His brief hope slipped away. "Bullshit. It won't let us go back down."

"The elevators go any which way for me. The Deviser has no use for me. It does for you."

"Why? You're the devoted disciple."

She laughed. "It's unaware of my devotion or your indifference. It may not know we even think or feel or emote. We're only potential cogs in its machine. Warped and useless, until it spent the last six thousand years forming us into exactly what it needs. Now a bit of final polish," Micah said as she gestured to the light through the mist, "and we're ready. Or you're ready, I should say. Not me. I don't fit into its machine."

Chris stood at the bottom of the hill of EXIT signs. He couldn't sprint up to Micah without his footing collapsing beneath him. He took a careful step forward. He needed to keep her talking. "What machine? What is it building?"

She laughed again. "We couldn't understand that any more than it can understand our minds. Maybe it's a great battleship to wage war against other Devisers. Maybe it's a bauble to amuse itself. It's not the first, and it won't be the last."

Chris climbed closer. She was ten feet away now. "There are other Devisers?"

"I don't know. I felt its mind, but all I recognized was desire."

"For us."

She shook her head. "To devise. To plan. To build. I recognized it because I share that desire. I've waited and watched, and now I've found the Deviser. It owes me what it gave those past architects and visionaries."

"It's done with gathering us. You just said so yourself. Now it's harvesting."

"It's building. Creating. But I've brought you here. That must count for something. I'm content to beg for scraps if the master's scraps will make me a legend. The only way I have to get its attention is to give it what it wants. More cogs. You." Micah hefted a piece of cinderblock from her shoulder bag.

"Stop calling the lurchers," Chris said. "They didn't take Leon or Dr. Terry. If those two men are now cogs like you say, it wasn't lurchers that took them."

Micah hesitated.

"You saw the building take Dr. Terry. The wall reached out and absorbed him. It wasn't a lurcher."

Chilled resolve filled her face. She ignored his reasoning to repeat her claims. "The Deviser will take you once you're nice and polished. I'll point to you with the lurchers."

Chris squeezed the paperweight. Micah had lost her mind.

Micah flung the piece of tile at Chris. It flew wide to bounce at the bottom of the pile of EXIT signs. Chris heard the hopping and dragging of lurchers behind him.

The calming effect of the light still reverberated through Chris's body and mind. He climbed the hill, the signs shifting under his feet.

From through the fog, Eddie yelled. "Dad!" Fear filled his cry, but not panic.

Chris told himself his boy was still okay.

Micah locked eyes with Chris. Through her madness, he

saw a remnant of her cunning ruthlessness. She pulled a doorknob from her bag and hurled it in Eddie's direction.

"No!" Chris leapt at the old woman. He swung the paperweight, bringing it down towards her hand, making contact only after she'd released her makeshift projectile.

Bones cracked. Skin broke. Bright blood splattered across the white and green EXIT signs.

Micah cried out and cradled her wounded hand. She stumbled down the hill towards Eddie.

Chris rode a landslide of EXIT signs to beat Micah to the bottom.

Even with her fit, muscled form, she now looked frail and vulnerable. But Chris's sympathy vanished when he saw the hateful determination in her gray eyes. She flung a brick at Chris's feet.

Chris grabbed her and dragged her away before the lurchers arrived to fix the floor.

She fought his grasp to pull a broken table leg from her bag. She reared back to throw it towards Eddie.

Chris again remembered Eddie's scream as he'd passed through the lurcher's pale, ethereal flesh.

He snatched the table leg from Micah and shoved her to the ground. She cried out as she hit the hard floor.

Chris stood over her, wooden spike in one hand, heavy glass club in the other.

Micah winced. With her good hand, she rubbed her hip. "You should embrace joining its machine. What option do you have? The Deviser wants you—the elevator won't let you back down. And I won't let you get back to it anyways. I'll point the lurchers to you before you make your way back."

Maybe he could still figure out how to make the Deviser

not want him, but not with Micah hunting them. Chris realized his only option. The calm that the light had injected into him was shaken. "You won't hurt my son."

"You can't stop me."

Chris raised the table leg.

Realization appeared on Micah's face. For all her billions of dollars, for all her magazine cover shoots, for all her pioneering of construction breakthroughs, her bones were just as brittle as any other sixty-year-old.

Chris broke the table leg over her knee.

Bone popped. Micah screamed. Something broke inside Chris. He'd done it to save Eddie, but he'd still intentionally inflicted violence on a defenseless old lady. He'd felt her kneecap give way through his grip on the table leg.

He tossed away the broken piece.

Micah's scream of pain turned to one of a wild fury. She hurled another brick into the fog. It didn't travel far. Spittle dripped down her chin. She dragged herself towards Eddie. She shrieked and growled like a cornered animal.

"Stop!" Chris ordered.

But Micah was determined, lashing out in a frantic, focused way. A lifetime of ambition now honed down into a single goal: hurt Chris by targeting his son.

Chris's stomach churned. He didn't know how long it would take them to find a way off this top floor. He couldn't leave Micah to crawl after them, appearing through the fog to hurt Eddie again. He hunched over the crawling old woman. He brought the paperweight down on her other knee, then he walked around her to smash her other hand. He felt her bones break.

He turned and threw up. He tried to think of anything

else, but his mind only replayed the sensation of Micah's bones breaking.

Micah screamed louder. The cunning in her eyes was gone. She ranted and spat hateful nonsense.

"I'm sorry," Chris whispered.

Micah slammed her face into the floor.

Chris jumped back.

She did it again.

Her nose shattered and flattened. A split above both eyes.

The tile floor cracked.

Chris backed away.

Micah swung her head down a third time, no doubt aiming to attract the lurchers as one final *fuck you* to Chris.

The sound of her skull cracking was louder than the tile cracking.

Micah's head drooped. She lay still.

Chris waited, watched for her back to rise and fall with the rhythm of breathing.

Nothing.

A single lurcher hopped and dragged itself out of the fog. It hunched over Micah.

Chris watched, wondering why it didn't go straight for the damaged tile.

The creature's blank face touched her knees, then her hands. It hopped to her head, hunched down, inspecting. It nudged her head around. Her body followed, yanked around by her neck. Micah stared lifelessly into the fog above. Blood pooled in her left eye. It ran down her cheek to paint her bleached teeth red.

The lurcher's face opened. Its tentacles reached out. They wriggled over Micah's eyes, spread out like a wet mop over her face. They continued to extend out of the lurcher, longer than Chris had seen before, thicker at their roots. They entered Micah's eyes, squeezing between the eyeball and the socket. They entered her nose, her mouth, her ears.

Chris couldn't understand what happened next.

Micah's leg stiffened and rose upwards like a Rockette marionette. It continued its arc to swing down against her chest. Into her chest. Out the other side. Her body grew ethereal to allow its passage, but not entirely. Liver, intestine, stomach were dragged along as her leg completed its rotation and started another.

Her torso lifted into a sit-up position, her head dangling behind. She folded into herself, down through the floor, rotation opposite to her legs. Her half-etherealness dragged tile, wiring, and steel studs up out of the floor, now merged with her flesh.

The lurcher hopped away, its repair job complete.

Chris backed away.

Micah's rotation stopped. Her hands rested on the floor. One sunk inches deep, like she was squatting in a puddle. A steel stud merged with her forearm, in one side and out the other at an angle. Sinew and muscle wrapped around it. Her major organs were outside her clothes, stitched to her body with pieces of tile and copper wires. Her head flopped to the side, shoulder and ear taking up the same space. A pipe stuck through her head, coming out of her eye. Nothing was static. She was a sludgy, shifting mass of flesh and building materials. She smelled of bile and shit and iron.

Her remaining eye opened. It was stained blood red. The pupil glittered.

She looked around.

Chris held his breath, afraid any movement would catch her attention.

Micah sobbed. Her nose slipped inside her face. Her whole face slid downward, then inside, then appeared at the top of her forehead. She gagged, Chris heard the liquid sound of vomit, and her neck ballooned to the side.

She worked her mouth, but her vocal cords were no longer linked to her lungs and tongue.

She crawled a step forward.

Pieces of the floor joined her.

Her heaving sobs turned to jerking spasms. She smashed a fist through the floor. Opened her mouth wide and shuddered, a silent scream of fury.

Chris stepped backwards.

If she touched him with her semi-ethereal form, it wouldn't be a moment of pain like the lurchers. It would be worse than when Leon had locked their fingers together. She would break him apart, make his pieces part of her. He feared his consciousness would survive.

Micah's head swung around. Her red eye and the open end of the iron pipe stared directly at him.

He ran.

59

─────────

CHRIS SPRINTED around the stack of rolled carpet to make his way back to Eddie and Roberts.

He found them twenty feet from where he'd left them. Roberts was standing again, eyes clear. Eddie clung to his leg, staring back where the lurchers had repaired the floor.

"Is she dead?" Roberts asked.

"Run," Chris yelled. "Back to the elevators. Swing around wide."

Roberts scooped up Eddie, who started to cry.

"It's okay, buddy," Chris ran alongside them. "We're going home. Keep your eyes closed."

"What happened?" Roberts asked.

They steered away from the cinderblock wall, back through the center of the room, into the fog.

"She was dead. A lurcher came and fixed her." Chris led them through a tunnel of plastic ferns. He relied on his sense of direction to point them back to the elevators.

Roberts held Eddie against his chest to keep his face away

from the ferns. "Why the elevators? They won't let us back down."

"Micah said it wouldn't let us down because the Deviser wanted us."

"Doesn't it still want us?"

They ran along the edge of the stacks of tile.

"Micah said it didn't want her. Figure out why, and we can get back down."

A furious, squelching scream filled the fog.

Eddie turned away from Roberts' chest. "What was that? Was that the lady?"

"Was it?" Roberts asked.

"Yes."

They circled the swamp of ink and ran past a maze of windows stood on their edges.

Micah screamed again, closer than before.

Chris saw the mountain of copy machines. "It's just up here." His lungs burned.

They reached the elevator bank, a squat cinderblock structure in the middle of the wide room. It made Chris think of the buildings he'd seen outside.

Two elevators. One door was open.

They stopped outside. Roberts set Eddie down. "How do we get it to let us down?"

"Micah said she could go up and down because it doesn't want her. What makes her different?"

"She worships the Deviser."

That didn't quite feel right to Chris.

Micah screamed again, from back the way they'd come. She was following their trail.

"I worshipped it, too," Roberts said. "Maybe it'll let me down if it's just me."

"You'll leave us up here?" Chris asked.

"Of course not," Roberts said. "I'll just send it down a floor. If it moves, I'll come right back up for you."

"And then it won't move with us."

"You'll say a prayer to the Deviser, and maybe it'll let you."

But Chris remembered Micah saying that the Deviser was hardly aware of them, unable to understand their thoughts or desires.

Micah screamed again.

"Do you have any better ideas?" Roberts asked.

Chris squeezed his eyes shut. Roberts' plan didn't make sense. It didn't fit the purpose of the building. It didn't fit their becoming cogs in the Deviser's machine. But Chris couldn't articulate what he was thinking.

Eddie backed away from the sound of Micah's approaching screams.

"I'm trying it." Roberts entered the elevator. He pushed the button. Nothing happened. "Maybe if I touch the wires together."

He fiddled with the bank of buttons.

Chris held Eddie tight. Despite the fear in Eddie's face, he didn't appear so broken down and turned inward like he had recently. If Chris could keep away his anxiety, and he could help Eddie stay happy and outgoing, then maybe the two of them could maintain a healthy family.

Everything clicked in Chris's brain.

The light that had cleared Chris's mind and cleared his anxiety—it powered the rooms below. The building polished minds, repaired people mentally and emotionally. Not people —cogs. It wasn't benevolent healing. Maybe "healing" wasn't even the right word. It was polishing them into what it needed.

The Deviser had spent millennia bringing people closer together, ready for harvest, and then determined that they weren't mentally fit enough to make its machine work. That's why this building was different than the others. It wasn't improving urban living—it wasn't part of the slaughterhouse funnel. It was seasoning on the steak. Or the final shaping of the cog before it slid into the machine.

The Deviser wasn't allowing Micah freedom—it was rejecting her. Not because she worshipped it, but because her mind was beyond repair.

"I think I've got it," Roberts said. "You know, once we get out of here, we should stay in touch. Even work together. I've seen how Micah's businesses run, and you've got talent. I feel like I've big things ahead of me."

Chris had heard those words before. "Get out of there!" he yelled.

Dr. Terry and Leon had that same delusion before they were taken. The epitome of mental health, or at least of this building's version of it: big things ahead.

Chris lunged to yank Roberts away from the walls of the elevator, but he was too slow.

An organic darkness bulged from the wall. It enveloped Roberts, sank into the floor, and was gone.

60

———

CHRIS FELT HIS SANITY SHAKING, but he wondered if it was enough.

He stared at the empty elevator.

"Dad?"

Chris looked down. He thanked any god that was listening that Eddie had been turned around and hadn't seen the building take Roberts.

"Dad?" he shrieked.

Micah crawled into view out of the fog. She was twelve feet tall now and at least as wide. Building materials now outnumbered her organs, but both formed a shifting hodge-podge in and on her warbling surface. Skin and drywall and veins and wiring. Her face had scattered throughout her form, but from the top and the bottom, a red eye and open pipe locked onto Chris.

He yanked Eddie into the elevator.

"Where's the other man?" Eddie whined.

Chris mashed the close-doors button. It didn't respond. The Deviser still wanted them.

Chris punched the wall. How could it still want them? Those fleeting seconds staring into the light weren't enough. This monstrosity dragging itself toward them—that had been his professional hero. And he'd turned her into this. He'd beaten a frail old woman to death. He could still feel the sensation of her knee popping and her wrist snapping.

Eddie pressed his face into Chris's side.

Terror filled Chris as he realized:

He was broken enough.

Eddie wasn't.

Whatever horrors Eddie faced, he could hide behind Dad.

Micah dragged herself closer. A limb of bone, sinew, and copper wire wobbled as it reached towards them.

"We can do it, Dad," Eddie whispered. "Let's go home, and you can design the biggest house in the world and the kids at school will want to come see it, but I'll only let the ones who are nice to me."

Chris shoved him away. "No!"

Eddie's mouth quivered in a frown. "Daddy?"

"I'm not your Dad! Your real mom didn't want you. Your new mom hated you so much she ran away."

Eddie cried.

Micah reached closer. Her bulk filled the doorway. A pumping lung scraped fiberglass insulation against the elevator doors' edge.

"You have to take care of me," Eddie cried. "You said."

"I lied."

"Say it again, but don't lie this time."

"It will always be a lie. I'll never take of you."

Eddie pushed himself against the wall. His mouth hung open. His eyes begged and accepted his loneliness at the same time. The monstrosity that was Micah bulged into the elevator, and Eddie was afraid of Chris.

Chris pressed the close-doors button again.

The doors slid closed, locking Micah out.

Chris pushed the button for the ground floor. The elevator moved. It took them downward.

Down a hundred and twenty floors. Chris didn't dare comfort Eddie. He didn't dare let himself show any emotion, to risk Eddie recognizing Chris's lie and becoming attractive to the Deviser again.

After a three-minute eternity, the elevator dinged. The doors opened.

It was the courtyard. Reflecting pool on one end. Checkerboard floor pattern, square planters, grass blowing in the breeze.

"Outside," Chris ordered. He grabbed Eddie's arm and ran.

They went through the dark vestibule and out the glass doors.

Police had cordoned off the block. Some part of Chris noticed them approaching, but he fell to his knees and wrapped Eddie in his arms. "I'm sorry. I lied upstairs. I'll never leave. I love you. I promise, I promise." He wept.

Eddie pulled away.

A teenage girl ran up to hug Eddie. "You made it!"

Eddie squeezed her tightly. "I thought the lady got you."

She noticed Chris. "You his dad?"

Chris nodded. He touched Eddie's cheek. "Look at me. The building wanted you. It would only let us go if you were sad. I had to make you sad. I'm so sorry. I'll never make you sad again. I promise."

Eddie looked at the girl, who said, "You know that building was fucked up. This guy loves you like my momma loves me. I can see that."

Eddie relented. He let Chris pick him up, and he lay his head on Chris's. But he remained stiff.

As news cameras pointed at them and a police officer approached, Chris exhaled.

He could work with this. As long as Eddie would give him a chance, he could spend the rest of his life proving to his boy that he loved him.

EPILOGUE

The FBI stopped calling after six months.

Chris told them everything that had happened, with the caveat that someone must have slipped him some magic mushrooms.

"I don't know what happened. I only know I went on a bad trip."

He left out the part where he'd mutilated an old woman. He didn't like remembering that part.

Chris, Eddie, and his friend Cam were the only ones to exit the building. Leon, Dr. Terry, and Roberts were listed as missing persons. Chris thought that description fit well. The Deviser had claimed them, and Chris had been powerless to help.

Micah Rayner was also listed as a missing person. That wasn't how Chris would describe her.

But the investigators never found her when they searched the building. Or at least, the first floor. The elevators refused to work, and the stairwells were sealed off.

Three weeks after the building appeared, it disappeared.

One moment it was there, the next it was gone. The news went crazy. Physicists wrote papers. Micah's corporate lackeys went on national news to invent cover stories for her disappearance.

That's when the FBI got really interested. But when they called again, Chris told them the same story. "I can't tell you what happened, only about the hallucinations."

He tried to stop them from interviewing Eddie, but he couldn't afford a lawyer. So he told Eddie to be honest. Eddie tried, but trauma was confusing. Eddie's stories to the interviewing agents did not stay the same. Details shifted. His friend Cam got beat up by a strange man. Then the next interview, his friend Cam beat up the strange man.

The best they could, they told the truth.

But Chris left out the key part: what he intended to do next.

His next life choices with Eddie weren't difficult.

He couldn't afford rent—he didn't dare go after Micah's corporation about the contract—so he went with his tail between his legs to his parents.

"We'd love to have you," his dad boomed over the phone. "I've been itching to show Eddie my new fishing boat."

There wasn't much architectural work to be found in Dumfries, Virginia. But Chris had a Master's, and that was enough to be a substitute teacher. He discovered he liked being "Mr. H," and watching the bulbs light up in kids' faces when they understood a new concept (that is, when the regular teacher didn't just leave him a movie to put on).

So his work and his living situation were last resorts that were turning out pretty well.

The FBI wouldn't care about any of that.

What Chris liked best about teaching was that he was off work when Eddie was home from school.

He often wished he could buy Eddie the gaming consoles and Lego sets he saw him eyeing on Youtube videos and in the stores. But that wasn't necessary. Eddie's new grandma and grandpa lived on ten acres of woods. Either during the three weeks they spent building a lincoln-log style fort, or during the two months they spent clearing a trail for their mountain bikes, Eddie relaxed more around Chris. He looked him in the eye again. He let Chris hug him for longer. He hugged back.

Chris still had nightmares about the building. The one that woke him up sweating and gasping was always about that last elevator ride down. When Chris convinced his son he was worthless.

Sometimes Chris peeked into Eddie's room after those nightmares. Eddie had a shelf full of books, a box of Chris's childhood toys, and an ever-growing pile of toys from grandma and grandpa. He slept like a rock.

For Eddie, the nightmare on the top floor was in the past. A little boy's mind was malleable. The lurchers, the impossible spaces, the thing that Micah had become—they weren't any scarier than memories of Ghostbusters cartoons. They couldn't hold a candle to his fears of being plucked away from his parents again.

Eddie connected with his grandparents. He rested on that foundation while Chris slowly built back what he'd destroyed.

But the FBI wouldn't care about any of that, either.

The thing the FBI would want to know about—which was exactly why Chris would never tell them—was what

Chris did on the Dumfries Public Library computers each morning before work. Fortunately, they didn't require a user login. And fortunately, they didn't block VPNs.

The first few weeks, Chris learned to make a bomb. Big enough to collapse a building. It was frighteningly easy. Not quite as easy if you needed it to be small enough to sneak in somewhere. But if Chris saw another building appear overnight, he had no intention of being sneaky.

He'd drive a truck into the lobby, walk away, and then set it off.

The more time passed, the more Chris decided he should try to get away with the crime, too. So he devised various plans.

After he learned how to make a bomb, his morning library ritual became much shorter. He checked his google alerts for anything suggesting another overnight building. He made friends in chatrooms—people who saw the Richmond building on the news and who were also watching for it to happen again.

And if it did, Chris would deal with it. He hoped it wouldn't happen in his lifetime. Or maybe never again. If the tower in Richmond was one link in a delicate chain of shepherding humans together, maybe failure meant it wouldn't try again.

Maybe the Deviser meant for Micah to build replicas. But Chris killed Micah—or rather, she killed herself after he left her for dead. No Micah, no replica buildings, no brain-tweaking slaughterhouses.

Chris hoped the chain had been broken.

But Chris still checked google and the chatrooms each morning.

After a year, he started to hope he was in the clear.

Then he got a text message from a blocked number. He hadn't even known that was possible.

"I know you witnessed Micah. I know you're watching for the Deviser."

Chris's heart froze. He was in class—American History, and the teacher had left Forest Gump on VHS, so he was sitting behind the desk in the dark while a class full of ninth graders played on their phones.

At first, Chris tried to ignore the text. He didn't know how to respond. Had the FBI found him through the VPN? Had they watched him at the library?

Then another text came through:

"Micah brought us together, but we didn't disband when the Deviser claimed her. We still seek the Deviser."

A whole cult just like Micah. Chris sank into his chair.

"I haven't told the others about you. They think you're an enemy. They think you tried to stop Micah from meeting the Deviser."

How did they have any clue what happened in the building? What did they want?

"If you got as close as Micah, then you must want to get back. I can't in good faith keep this hidden from you..."

Chris stared at his phone, waiting for the next message, not wanting to see it.

"The cruise liner *The Aria of the Seas* appeared overnight on the ocean. It was given to mankind like the Deviser's other gifts. The cruise company found it and is switching it out with an older *Aria of the Seas* that was about to be decommissioned."

Chris had only been looking for buildings. It never

occurred to him that the Deviser could send a boat. He couldn't drive a car bomb onto a cruise ship. Could he?

"Our organization will be on the new ship's first voyage in three weeks. If you want to reconnect with the Deviser, you should be there, too. But please remember, the others in our organization will see you as an enemy. Keep a low profile. I just couldn't live with myself if I didn't give you this opportunity. I had to help you get back to the Deviser."

These guys still thought the Deviser was a happy bearded god, sending his obedient children architectural rewards. Chris didn't want to be anywhere where he might risk seeing that flat, infinite plane again. Or risk getting snatched away like Leon or Dr. Terry or Roberts.

But he couldn't let an ignorant cult help the Deviser get another foothold in this reality.

Chris found the *Aria of the Seas* on the cruise line's website. As promised, it was currently undergoing work, but the next voyage was in three weeks.

Chris bought a ticket.

He had a ship to sink.

THE HORROR CONTINUES in **Book Two: They Cling to the Hull**

<<<<>>>>

FROM THE AUTHOR

Thanks for reading *It Waits on the Top Floor*. The horror continues in *They Cling to the Hull*.

For more cosmic horror, check out my novel *The Piper's Graveyard*, and my short fiction collection *Crowded Chasms: Tales of Weird Horror*.

If you like action & adventure with your Lovecraftian nightmares, you might enjoy novel *Those Who Dwell Below the Sidewalk*.

For a free horror novella, visit my website: BenFarthing.com